A
THOUSAND
AWKWARD MOMENTS

A
THOUSAND
AWKWARD MOMENTS

Marie Dunn

iUniverse, Inc.
Bloomington

A Thousand Awkward Moments

iUniverse books may be ordered through booksellers or by contacting:

iUniverse
1663 Liberty Drive
Bloomington, IN 47403
www.iuniverse.com
1-800-Authors (1-800-288-4677)

ISBN: 978-1-4759-6156-0 (sc)
ISBN: 978-1-4759-6158-4 (hc)
ISBN: 978-1-4759-6157-7 (ebk)

Library of Congress Control Number: 2012921695

Printed in the United States of America

iUniverse rev. date: 12/12/2012

CHAPTER 1

Looking back, a blind man could see what I missed, but a blind man doesn't trust his *eyes* for the truth. He believes what he *can't* see. He relies on his other senses—what he can smell, hear, taste, and feel. In reality, people only see what they choose to see.

*   *   *

We had been standing in the visitation line for two hours. The crowd was buzzing with different theories about Mr. Dutton's death. Apparently, he had gone into the hospital for a simple procedure, some said kidney stones, others said gallbladder, and had died. It was all hush-hush, and the family had been paid not to discuss the details of his death. Gary Dutton was the school superintendent. Out of respect, I knew we should give our condolences to his family, but really, I couldn't even see the end of the line. The temperature had risen from ninety-four to ninety-nine degrees since we'd been standing on the hot concrete drive outside the church, and my new heels were shrinking a size for every hour we stood in line. As an elementary school teacher, I didn't dress up that often. I knew we would run into people I had not seen in years, so I wore my conservative, little black dress that hugged my curves and, unfortunately, held in all the heat. The neckline was perfect to show off my black pearl necklace. My blonde hair was in a loose updo that accentuated my teardrop pearl earrings. The little straps on my new skin-tone heels were digging into my toes, and I felt a blister forming on my right heel. When I had left the house, I felt confident and thought I looked hot, but after standing in the blistering August sun, I was just hot and irritated. My patience was failing.

I looked up at my husband, Don, to see how he was faring with the heat. He worked out, religiously, every day at 4:30 a.m. He was six feet tall with light brown hair, blue eyes, and a runner's body. He was used to long bike rides and running in the heat, so, even though I could see sweat dripping from his temples, he wasn't terribly bothered by the heat.

We had exhausted the conversation with the peripheral crowd standing near us in line. I debated how much longer I could stand in my heels, when I noticed a couple, who had reached their tolerance for the heat, walking arm in arm back down the hill to their car.

"Do you want to go?" I asked my husband.

"You can go, Diane, but I'm staying," he replied curtly.

He said it with such conviction that I was taken aback. I didn't know whether to feel guilty, hurt, or curious, but his no-nonsense tone suggested there would be no more discussion about it, so I shuffled through the procession for two more agonizing hours.

When we were within three people of the widow, Carol Dutton, she looked my husband straight in the eye and beamed with such exuberance that it felt as if she had just seen a loved one step off a plane.

She all but pushed the few people in front of us out of the way, looked at me, and asked, "Can I give your husband a hug?"

I was so bewildered that I sputtered, "Of course," and also gave her a quick hug as well.

She responded with a dismissing giggle, "Oh . . . okay."

It was so awkward; she seemed startled by my hug. She proceeded to introduce my husband to her son and daughter. The scene quickly turned into a cocktail party atmosphere; it was a surreal moment. Without being included in the introductions, I just stood there like an onlooking bystander. They were all smiles and told him that they had heard so much about him. They continued sharing stories about working out together at the gym and discussing how much my husband sweats during spinning class.

Carol turned to me, at one point, and asked, "Who does his laundry?"

I replied, "I do," but thought, *What the hell kind of question is that?* I chided myself for the thought; no one should be judged for what she says when her dead husband is lying behind her.

The people behind us were becoming irritated at the amount of time we were taking up; I could feel their stares and hear their silent pleas begging us to keep moving. But Carol just kept talking and making more leading comments to keep us engaged in conversation. I was so uncomfortable that I gently nudged my husband to move through the line, while Carol kept making more small talk. I just wanted to go home. I had to keep adjusting the strap on my shoe to keep it off the blister, making it hard to walk. We had stood in the sweltering sun, on a hot concrete walk for the last four hours, and I couldn't put an end to that awkward conversation fast enough. I didn't know Don had known them that well.

Don was an architect for a firm in town. The firm was located on the west side of Springfield, Illinois, about a twenty-minute drive from our house. He had worked for the firm for almost twenty-five years. He had been working on a project that seemed like a house of cards, because it was late-night phone calls and nonstop trips back into the office on weekends to keep the project on schedule and from falling apart. He must have left his phone elsewhere that day, because it was the first time in months I could remember being together for more than an hour without his phone interrupting.

On the way home, my husband seemed unusually reticent when I attempted to discuss the exchange we'd just had with Carol and her kids. I asked about them working out together, because she looked remarkably slim. Carol was a special-education teacher. It was as if she had a complete makeover. She had probably dropped more than fifty pounds, her hair had been dyed blonde, she wore makeup, and she was dressed very youthful, bordering on sexy. It was a stark contrast from the hefty woman with thick, brown, helmet-styled hair and no makeup that she was a few years ago.

When I first met her, I was selling real estate, and she came to my open house. We introduced ourselves and realized our daughters were the same age and that her husband, Gary, was my daughter, Anna's, principal at the time.

Gary had been a terrific guy. I was tearfully upset at the family's loss. Her son was in college, and her daughter would also be leaving for college in a few weeks. It was hard to imagine waking up one day after twenty-plus years of marriage to an empty house with the kids in college knowing your husband wasn't coming back. I had been looking forward to the day when our lives weren't scheduled around ball games and high school activities. I wondered if they had looked forward to their time alone. I started thinking about her husband and the last time I saw him.

*   *   *

It was in my classroom a few months ago in May. I had just walked to the back of the room to stop two students who were shoving each other over whose turn it was at the computer, when who walked in but Mr. Dutton, the county superintendent, and my principal. Surprise! My mind started racing through questions. *What are they doing here? How long are they going to stay? What in the hell are they doing in my room at eight on a Monday morning?* I mean, usually our principal gave us a day's notice when the superintendent would be in the building, so I knew it was a surprise to her, as well.

I said, "Hello," as I smiled and shook his hand. "Welcome to my classroom."

I started to share what the kids were working on, but he cut me off in midsentence and said, "I saw your husband this morning."

I was so shocked. I just wasn't expecting the conversation to turn to a personal note. I was trying to follow what he was saying, but, honestly, all I was thinking was, *Jacob is still fighting with Lindsay about the damn computer. Oh, great, Marcus is ripping paper for spit wads! I can't even hear him over Jill sharpening her pencils!* He was still talking about seeing my husband and seemed to be asking me a question. *Crap, what did he say?*

Not sure of what he asked, I responded by asking, "Are you part of that crazy group my husband works out with at four thirty in the morning?"

He laughed, and we continued small talk for another five minutes; however, it felt as if it was another hour.

The last words I heard him say were, "You really need to find out where your husband goes in the morning." He laughed and walked out of my room.

I politely laughed and felt relieved when they were gone, so that I could refocus my attention on the students.

*   *   *

My thoughts were interrupted back to the present when I saw Jack, our black Lab, sitting near the road at the end of our half-circle drive, *outside* the invisible fence. He looked so happy to see us and was jumping on the car.

Urrr, we will have to repaint this car if we want any resale because of the claw marks going down the car doors.

I was mad at Don every time those dogs jumped on the car. He had promised to train them when he insisted we needed two black Labs for the property. We had built our dream home in the country. The large Cape Cod brick home sat in front of a wooded pond. Trails cut through the woods and over a creek that led to a small pasture. A fence separated our pasture from several huge horse pastures belonging to the farmer several miles away.

The dogs had the run of the two-acre perimeter around the house that was enclosed by an invisible fence. Jill, the female black Lab, was two when she joined Jack, who was a puppy, four years ago. They were to be outside dogs that slept in the garage, although Jill, who had been an inside dog up until the time she arrived at our house, wasn't pleased to be burdened with a puppy or expected to be outside. She wasn't very nice to Jack, to say the least.

Jack was still sitting at the end of the drive looking forlornly at us to help him. I knew when he didn't follow us up to the garage that the dogs had been running the perimeter, and Jill had herded Jack to the outside and then pushed him through the invisible fence. It was her favorite way to seek some peace from Jack. She was sitting in the afternoon sun, alone on the back porch, very content, until she saw us pull into the drive. Irritated, she stretched, yawned, and strolled to the backyard. I slipped on some flip-flops and walked back down the lane, took off Jack's shock collar and tried to drag him over the invisible fence line. He wouldn't budge. I yelled at Don to start the Gator. Jack loved to ride around the property in the Gator. So when Don drove down the lane, Jack jumped in the back and went for a ride before I put his shock collar back on inside the perimeter.

Just as I clicked Jack's collar and he raced to seek his revenge on Jill, Anna pulled in the drive after working in town that morning at Panera.

"Tell me you didn't wear those shoes with that dress!" gasped Anna.

"No, Anna. My heels gave me a blister, and I haven't had a chance to change."

We walked into the kitchen, and she ran upstairs to change her clothes. Anna was a beautiful girl with blonde hair, big brown eyes, and the perfect teenage body. She was very athletic and had started at softball, volleyball, and basketball since her freshman year.

Anna called down from upstairs, "Mom, can I go to the afternoon movie? It starts in forty-five minutes."

Before I could answer, Anna's friend, Shelby, ran in the back door sprinting from Jack and Jill, who were chasing her from her car.

"Hey, is Anna ready?" Shelby asked breathlessly.

"Can I, Mom?" asked Anna, coming down the stairs. "Shelby's driving, and we're picking up Becky on the way."

"When will you be home?"

"After the movie. Mom, we gotta go now!" Anna replied, exasperated.

"All right," I agreed, and before I could say anything else, they were out the door with Jack and Jill close behind.

As the girls pulled out of the drive, Don walked in and asked where Anna was going. I proceeded to give him the rundown on the girl's plans, but I could tell he wasn't paying any attention.

"I think I'm going in to the office to finish some things that I didn't have a chance to work on this morning. I'll be back later," Don said nonchalantly.

*   *   *

I went to change my clothes and started to analyze the whole visitation experience again. It was just so awkward. I wasn't an expert on visitations, but *who asks about dirty laundry in a receiving line?*

The phone interrupted my thoughts. I looked at the number and answered, "Hey, what's goin' on?"

It was my twin sister, Ellen; she wanted to know if we'd gone to the visitation. I told her that we had and filled her in on the strange details of the conversation.

She responded sarcastically, "Well, don't you think she was being a little *too* familiar with *your* husband?"

I was impervious to Ellen's insinuations. She truly believed men were incapable of being faithful. She was passionate about looks and clothes. Her favorite quote was "If the barn needs painting, paint it!" I believed in staying fit, but not if it involved pain or getting up at 4:30 a.m. to work out. I didn't judge anybody if that is what they wanted, but my small athletic build was fine with me; nor did I live a lifestyle where that really mattered.

I ignored her tone and relayed that the Duttons worked out at the gym with Don in the mornings.

With equal sarcasm, she asked, "Well, do you think that's all there is to it?"

We had had versions of that conversation so many times throughout the years. I had always told her that if my husband cheated on me, I didn't want to know, because, in my mind, it would be a fling, and he should have to live with the guilt. She, on the other hand, had many different scenarios of crushing testicles and devious forms of revenge.

I could tell she wasn't going to let it go; she had something she was bound and determined I was going to hear.

So I asked, "What *more* are you implying?"

I trusted Don. We had been married for twenty-three years. He had been the head usher at church for the last ten years. He taught weekly Bible study, and the nuns were frequently tasking him to stand in as a pallbearer or for different church needs. Don was not the type of man who would cheat.

"Well, do you *really* want to know?" Ellen asked, impertinent.

By then, I was fed up with her games and told her, "If you have something to say, *say it!*"

She responded, "Are you sure you want to know? Do you really want to know? 'Cause if you really want to know, I'll tell you." Ellen was adamant for verbal assurance, so she could say later that *I* wanted to know.

My stomach dropped at that point. I could tell that it was more than an insinuation, and my curiosity was getting the better of me.

I finally blasted back, *"If you've got something to say, say it!"* Her next words changed my entire life.

Ellen took a deep breath and exhaled, "Don's having an affair. And it's been going on for over a year."

I thought, *Okay, more gossip. Why is she doing this?*

"How do you know that?" I asked defensively.

Ellen proceeded to tell me about different rumors she and her husband, Keith, had heard. "Terry, Keith's cousin, was over last week, and he said, 'What kind of marriage does your sister have? Her husband can't keep his hands off this one woman at the health club, and it's embarrassing to even work out around them. Everyone is talking about it.' I told him that you didn't know anything about it."

What? I don't even know Terry. He probably doesn't even know who Don is.

"When I told him that you didn't suspect Don, he was like, 'How can she not know? It's been going on for a year!' and I told him that you didn't go to the health club."

Going on over a year? That's impossible! Don comes home every night.

Ellen said, "And Kelli, our sister-in-law, called me the other day and said a friend of hers called her and told her basically the same thing. She wanted me to tell you."

Why didn't Kelli tell me? Why are they all telling Ellen? There must be some truth to this if all these people are talking.

I started to wonder what Don had done to start these kinds of rumors when I asked, "If they're having an affair, where do they meet?"

He comes home every night; I can't imagine he has time to meet a woman.

"At the health club," Ellen said, as if I hadn't been listening.

But that group has met for years. It's just a bunch of guys.

Ellen shook my foundation when she said, "I confronted him about it last November. He denied all the rumors, and we had a big fight about it. Don told me, 'You need to mind your own business, Ellen. You're just spreading gossip that doesn't have any truth to it.'"

Don had told her what I was thinking.

"I told him, 'Okay, if there isn't anything to the rumors, then why don't you tell Diane about them? Put an end to them? You could clear the air.'"

Why wouldn't he have told me if he didn't have anything to hide?

Ellen mimicked Don, saying, "He told me, 'There's no reason to bring Diane into these rumors and hurt her that way.'"

I did notice they haven't been that close . . .

Ellen said, "I threatened him, at that point, that if I heard anymore rumors, I was going to tell you."

It's funny how your brain processes shocking information. All I heard was that *she confronted him last November,* and all I could think was *why didn't you tell me then?*

Ellen continued, "And when I told Mom, she said that Anne had heard the rumors too."

Mom and both my sisters, Anne and Ellen, knew? My whole family knows and was at my house for Christmas. Didn't it occur to anybody to say something to me?

I was still trying to process what she was telling me, but my brain kept getting hijacked on details, and I had to have her repeat the sordid details again.

"Where did you say they meet, again?" I asked, trying to force the information to stick in my brain.

"They meet in the morning; evidently, they are the first ones at the health club, and the janitor lets them in early," Ellen said, as if the janitor was part of a conspiracy.

Again, bells and horns were sounding in my head. I was processing little bits of information at a time. By then, the vortex of information was starting to form a pattern, but I just couldn't quite piece it together yet.

Words were starting to coalesce when I said, "Wait! What did you say about a woman at the health club? What is her name?"

Ellen's answer felt like a boulder had just dropped on me as the realization of it all hit me. The next words out of Ellen's mouth literally made me lose my balance and have to sit down.

When I asked Ellen what the name of this woman was, she said, "I don't know her name, but I heard she just lost her husband, and they work out together at the health club."

I was speechless. It all made sense. *How could I have been so clueless?*

"Did you know it was her when I went to the funeral?" I asked, dumbfounded.

"No, I suspected, but I only knew for sure when you told me her reaction to Don."

I just couldn't believe it, but at the same time, so many things were speeding into place. I hung up the phone and went outside to sit in the sun on the back porch. Jack came running up and nuzzled me under the arm until his head was poking through to my lap, and before I knew it he was rolled over in my lap for a belly rub. He hadn't figured out yet that he wasn't still a little puppy. I was so numb from the information I'd just received that I let Jack comfort me with his warm fur and affection. I sat there for over an hour and scratched his tummy and rubbed his ears, until I heard a car pulling into the drive.

*　　*　　*

Jack and Jill hit the drive the minute they heard the sound of tires on the gravel. I looked up to see Anna's car pull into the drive after the movie. I quickly made up my mind that I was going to keep the new information to myself until I had a chance to digest it. My stomach dropped as I heard the next car pull in the drive, but it was Anna's friends. The girls scurried out of their car before the dogs started jumping on their car doors. I called Jack and Jill to me with treats, so the girls could go inside without the dogs jumping on them. After the girls were inside, I decided to walk out to the garden to see if there were any fresh tomatoes to make BLTs. I was still mulling over the information Ellen had told me about Carol and Don. I kept thinking about all the times Don said he had been working, questioning everything he had ever told me.

Did they sleep in my bed? Where did they meet? How long has this been going on? How did it start? Had her husband known? When was the last time Don and I had sex?

I started to freak out, but realized I needed to keep it together for one more week until Anna left for college. I would figure out what I was going to do once she was settled at SIU, Southern Illinois University. I picked a few tomatoes and some green beans and went back inside. I had just finished washing and snapping the green beans when I heard the garage door. It felt as if time were moving in slow motion, because I was analyzing his every word and action. I could hear him coming in the back door. My stomach was in my throat. I wondered where he'd been. My hands started shaking with anger. I didn't look at him for fear of giving away my information.

He nonchalantly asked, "What are we having for dinner?" as if nothing was wrong.

"BLTs with green beans from the garden," I replied, trying to sound casual.

Everything felt and sounded normal; *maybe Ellen doesn't know what she is talking about.* I had to fight the urge to just ask him about Carol and see what he was going to say. *No, I'm not going to create a scene until I have more information, and we are alone. What the hell, after twenty-three years of marriage, and now I feel as if Don is a total stranger.* He was in the bedroom changing his clothes when the girls came downstairs and headed for the pond to sunbath on the dock.

Don came into the kitchen and asked, "Did we get any mail?"

It was so surreal having these completely routine conversations with him while, on the inside, I was freaking out with questions, curiosity, and overwhelming betrayal.

"Not much, mostly junk mail; it's on the desk, if you want to look at it," I said calmly.

"No, I'll be down the basement working on Anna's loft for her dorm room; holler at me when dinner is ready," he said, eager to head downstairs.

I just kept toasting bread and frying bacon. I had toasted an entire loaf of bread and fried a whole package of bacon before I realized I'd better ask Anna if her friends Shelby and Becky were staying for dinner.

We laughed and were entertained by Anna's and her friends' stories over dinner. Don and the girls went downstairs after dinner to check out the progress on the loft while I stacked the dishwasher and put the leftover bacon in the dog's dish. By the time the kitchen was clean, the girls had come up from the basement and were making plans to go out for the evening. They parted ways to change and were going to meet later. I really didn't trust myself to be alone with Don. I sat down, turned on the TV, and pretended to be absorbed in a show. I couldn't have told you what show was on TV. My mind was trying to go down so many paths, at the same time that I couldn't hold one single thought. I decided to take a hot shower, hoping that would calm my frayed nerves. I should have jumped in the shower after I'd been in the garden, anyway.

Later, Becky came back to pick up Anna. She was also going to SIU, and we were discussing moving details, when Don came up from the basement.

"Hey, Bec, what are you all dressed up for?" he asked, upbeat.

"Nothing, we're just going to hang out at Keely's house tonight," replied Becky. Don just accepted her answer.

As far as I was concerned, he couldn't even breathe right at that point; anything and everything he did set me off.

I knew Becky was full of it; she was extremely dressed up to hang out at Keely's house. I knew I should have asked more questions at that point, but I just didn't have the energy to follow through on trying to finagle the real truth of where they were going, and all the cajoling that would ensue. I figured they were leaving in a few days, and hopefully they wouldn't get caught at whatever they were up to. I gave Anna an absolute time she had to be home by, and then I let it go. She probably didn't argue with the curfew, because I wasn't asking fifty questions about where she was going.

After the girls left, Don went back downstairs to work on the loft. As I sat there pondering my next move, the questions were thundering in my head. The only way the scores of questions swirling in my head would be answered was to ask him the truth. I had decided I'd just go downstairs under the guise of checking out the loft's progress, and I'd casually bring up the health club and Carol. I would gauge his reaction and continue from there.

When I went downstairs, I sat on the bench press that was part of Don's workout equipment. I felt the emotional temperature drop twenty degrees; it was obvious he didn't want me down there.

"What's up?" he asked curtly.

"Nothing. I just wanted to see how the loft was coming. Do you think it'll be finished before tomorrow?" I asked, trying to sound nonchalant.

"I'm not going to finish it here. I'm just going to put together the basic parts so that all the nuts and bolts are attached. I'll keep the main structures unassembled, so they will pack flat in the bottom of the U-Haul."

"That makes sense. So then you're basically done with what you need to do for the loft now, right?"

"Yeah. I have another hour or so to just sand down some of the edges and do some finishing work, but it'll be done tonight."

There was an uncomfortable pause, and then I blurted out, "So who all works out at the health club in the mornings?" *Smooth . . .*

"Same people as always," he responded derisively.

"Does Carol still work out there in the mornings?" I asked as my heart started racing.

"Sometimes," he said tentatively.

"So how well do you know Carol?" I thought, *I'm going for it,* as my voice went up an octave and became accusatory.

"Well, real well," he replied defiantly.

He just kept his head down and was fidgeting with the loft. I just kept thinking, *I want to know the truth,* and persevered toward finding it.

I decided to just be direct and asked him straight out, "Are you having an affair with her?"

He looked me straight in the eye and spit out, "I'm not having this conversation with you until Anna leaves for college."

With those words, my world started to crumble. He said more in what he *didn't* say, than what he *did* say. He was, actually, saying that he'd been thinking about how to tell me that he was having an affair, and that he'd been waiting for Anna to leave to tell me. He was just sitting there, looking at me, waiting for a response.

I looked at him and shot back, "Oh yes, you are! We've been married for twenty-three years, and you owe me the truth! You are going to tell me *exactly* what is going on," I said, escalating toward full-on bitch mode.

"Who told you?"

"Apparently, the whole fucking town knows! You've been seen making out all over the place, and everyone in town, and at the health club, is talking about it!" I screamed.

I realized my voice was reaching an extreme decibel level. I knew the discussion would soon be over if I didn't pull myself together.

He just kept repeating, "I'm not having this conversation with you. I'm not having it."

I finally said in a calm voice, "Look, I'm not wanting to fight. I just want to know the truth. This doesn't need to be a scene. Are you having an affair with Carol?"

His response was "I love her. She is my soul mate. We are going to get married."

Never in a million years did I think *that* was going to come out of his mouth. I thought there would be groveling; he'd cry, tell me that we could go to counseling, we'd work on the marriage, all sorts of other scenarios—*not that.*

At first, my initial response was to crack up laughing. It just seemed hysterical to me that he actually used the cliché "she is my soul mate." He was looking at me as if *I* were hysterical. Random thoughts floated through my mind: *let her do your disgusting laundry . . . smell your putrid gym shoes . . . watch boring sports . . . and tolerate your disgusting habits.* That didn't seem like what I should be thinking; maybe I *was* cracking up. I should be feeling sad. It was like an out-of-body experience. I was hearing the tragic news passing between us, but I just found everything he said so amusing. *What the hell is wrong with me?*

As we talked, he continued to open up about his affair, even though he would never call it that. He would only acknowledge that he loved her and they were meant to be.

I asked, "So what are you thinking? How is this all going to play out? What are you and your *soul mate* planning? What about this house? The dogs? What are you thinking?"

"We'll work it all out. You've been a good wife and mother; this is just something that happened. I didn't plan it. I love her. She gets me."

At that point, I thought I was going to barf. *Who is this ass sitting here in front of me?* I was *so* done listening to his crap.

As I went upstairs, I reminded him about Sunday dinner.

*   *   *

Every Sunday afternoon, both of our parents would come over for a potluck-style dinner. My mom and mother-in-law, Mary, would coordinate the salad and dessert, and we would fix the main course and side dishes. Dinner was at five o'clock. Mom and Mary would help clean the kitchen after dinner while Dad and Roger would often check the progress of the garden or settle around a game on TV. We had done that for the last three or so years. They were always entertained by Anna's rotation of boyfriends at the dinner table. I recognized that if the situation proceeded to a divorce, it was going to affect so many more people other than just us. I chastised myself for that thought and told myself, *We are not going to get a divorce.*

Later, after Anna was home and Don had gone to bed, I walked through the house turning off lights, admiring the rich colored wood floors along with the oversized woodwork and moldings throughout each room. We had duplicated those found in the historic district of town. The moon was reflecting off the pond and coming through the wall of windows that stretched the entire back of the house. The simple beauty of the pond inspired a sense of awe and a desire to whisper a silent prayer of gratitude for my beautiful home. It was a spiritual feeling the way the woods and animals communed with us in that space. For me, it was as if I could sense a gentle spirit with us that seemed pleased at how we had provided a comfortable home for all who shared the property. My father-in-law had planted an extensive garden on the edge of the woods that our furry friends enjoyed, much to his continual defenses. The pond had been drained, expanded, and restocked with new fish. The perimeter of the pond had been planted with various trees, plants, and foliage that created a small wetland and habitats for indigenous animals and birds. The change of seasons created magnificent scenery to enjoy from the comfort of our home.

As I walked into my closet, I looked around at the large center island that had an abundance of drawers and storage. One side of the closet was dedicated to Don, and the other walls were equipped with shoe racks and intricate wall organizers. I loved organization. The closet had truly been a reflection of my life. When I woke up that morning, I had everything I wanted in its organized place. I had felt truly comfortable and in control of my life. As I stared in the mirror, I questioned who I saw, as my entire life had changed in that one day. My thoughts ruminated over the luxury of my master bath. It was my favorite room of the house. I had spent hours poring over the house plans to create my private oasis. I had chosen floor-to-ceiling, dresser-styled cabinets with a long granite double-sink vanity. Wonderful-smelling candles, scented bath soaps, and assorted spa items surrounded the luxurious soaking tub. Even my spa-inspired bath couldn't provide the solace I needed. I was thinking about my deceased grandma's words, *"The only thing certain in life is change,"* when my thoughts were interrupted by Anna yelling down from upstairs, "Mom, did you wash my work clothes?"

Hmph! All thoughts were postponed for another day when I left the solitude of my closet, started a load of wash, and wrote a note to myself to throw them in the dryer first thing in the morning.

*   *   *

The next afternoon Ellen was over, and we were sitting around the kitchen talking and watching the kids run from the dogs and play in the pond. Anna and her friends were sunbathing on the dock. I loved watching all the kids play in the pond. My nieces and nephews had their little life jackets on and were taking turns jumping off the diving board from the dock. Jake, Anna's friend, was dangling Ethan, my five-year-old nephew, by his feet and threatening to drop him in the water. Ethan was squealing with delight, until Jake actually threw him into the pond. I watched him surface from the water, climb the ladder, and taunt Jake all over again, until Jake picked him up and held him over the water—as goes the "again game."

"Well, what happened last night? Did you confront Don?" asked Ellen cautiously.

"I did. Anna was gone, so I asked him about Carol and working out," I said solemnly.

"He denied it, didn't he? He is such a fucking liar," seethed Ellen.

"No, he said she was his soul mate and that they were going to get married."

Ellen looked as if I had slapped her. Neither of us said anything as we watched the kids play in the pond.

After a while, Ellen asked, "So what are you going to do?"

I looked at her clueless and sighed, "Put one foot in front of the other and keep moving forward. After Anna is settled at college, I'll think about how I'm going to figure out this mess."

CHAPTER 2

Friday, August 10. Moving day.

The U-Haul was packed and hitched behind the car. We were on our way to Southern Illinois University. Anna was excited, but I could tell she was having some anxious moments when she left her room. She was in her closet, which was bigger than her dorm room, looking through the window that overlooked the pond. She was watching the dogs playing tug-of-war with a bear-sized chew bone that Don had given them to keep them occupied for the day.

She asked in a small voice, "Who is going to take care of the dogs while we're gone?"

I assured her, "Grandpa will check in on them; they'll be fine overnight."

I could tell she was missing them already. As we walked out of her room, she gave one last look around the room.

*   *   *

The three-hour trip down to SIU was, actually, surprisingly pleasant. We laughed and talked about what we were going to do when we arrived on campus. Don and I were staying the night at the Holiday Inn. The following day we planned to set up bank accounts for Anna and run last-minute errands. We listened to music and had normal conversations as if nothing was out of the ordinary. I felt hopeful that the weekend would realign Don's priorities. I was sure he would come to the conclusion that he was having a midlife crisis of some sort, and that he would snap back to reality.

*   *   *

When we arrived at the dorm, it was a mob scene. There were cars, trailers, students, and parents everywhere. Several young men were at the curb of the dorm to help and direct the freshmen into their new surroundings. Within the first five minutes of us pulling into the unloading zone, Anna had met three hunky, good-looking sophomore boys, and they were directing her to her new dorm room, loaded with boxes. Don and I shared a knowing look, as we knew, all too well, the attention Anna drew. The moment passed, and he began hauling out boxes and following the boys to the dorm room. I stayed with the car until most of the U-Haul and car were unpacked, and we could move out of the unloading zone to a regular parking spot. Then I went to check out Anna's new digs.

If I had thought the parking lot was crazy, the dorm was even crazier. The elevators were crammed full of moving boxes, so the only choice was to join the masses in the hot, crowded staircase and walk up the eleven flights of stairs. When I reached her room, her roommate, Stacy, and her parents were there. We went through the introductions while the girls worked out which side of the room they each wanted, and Don began setting up the loft. Stacy seemed like a nice girl. She was tall with dark hair and a bad complexion. She had a strong Chicago accent. They were from Schaumburg, a suburb of Chicago. She wasn't sure what she was going to major in yet, but neither did Anna. Anna had picked SIU because it was known for the parties, and it was the farthest she could be from home and still be in Illinois. I was gathering Stacy had the same "career goals" after talking to her parents.

After Don assembled the loft, we began unpacking and organizing Anna's side of the dorm room. By late afternoon, the heavy work and most of the unpacking were done, and we started getting on each other's nerves when we weren't agreeing how things should be put away. That's when I knew we should head out for the evening. It was her room. I was tired and ready to check into the hotel before we met up with Becky's parents, Alan and Dawn Stone. The girls wanted to stay at the dorm and order pizza for dinner, so we said our good-byes to Stacy's parents and the girls and headed for the hotel.

When we arrived at the hotel, everything was going along fine until he said, "I can't get any reception on my phone. I'm going to step outside to check my work messages."

We'd had such a good day; I just didn't want to start anything by making accusations about the phone call. I unpacked, changed my clothes, touched up my makeup, and waited for him to come back to the room. The room had two double beds. He had put his bag on the one closest to the window. We had never slept apart in twenty-three years. *Is he going to sleep in the other bed?* We were meeting the Stones in thirty minutes, and I refused to upset myself over that before we left. I could hear Don's key in the door, so I brushed all thoughts of the phone call away and decided to have a good time at dinner.

*　　*　　*

At the restaurant, the Stones were already there. They were in the bar area and were each sipping on a beer. We joined them at the bar and ordered drinks. We began swapping the day's stories of the girls' moving day adventures. We were laughing and really enjoying ourselves, when Dawn asked if we had any fun plans, now that Anna would be away at school. I took a sip of my drink and was rescued from having to answer her by the waitress, who said that our table was ready.

At the table, we were all talking and joking about different things when Dawn said teasingly, "You know a lot of couples go their separate ways once the kids are in college. Statistics show that couples get divorced when they are left alone with their spouses after the kids are gone." She was laughing.

Alan teased her back, "I may not be able to stand you, now that we're alone, Dawn; we might be part the statistics."

I didn't hear a word she said after statistics. *Did she know about Don's affair? I don't think she did, because Alan started carrying the divorce joke right along with Dawn.* It was so awkward. I could tell Don was uncomfortable as well, because he hadn't said one word. They finished their beers and ordered another round; I was still nursing my drink when the waitress asked us if we were ready to order. I couldn't tell you what I ordered or what it tasted like. My thoughts had been hijacked back to the real world. I started wondering if it would be the last meal we shared with someone else as a couple, and from that moment on, everything we did, I questioned whether it would be the last time.

Back at the hotel, we were getting ready for bed. We were each in separate beds watching TV. We hadn't mentioned the conversation with the Stones, and I really didn't think he wanted to discuss our circumstances anymore than me, at that point. I had a dry lump in my throat at the realization that it might be the last time we spent a weekend together as a family. Tears were stinging my eyes at the thought of it.

Don asked, "Are you watching this show? If not, I'm going see what is on the other channels."

"That's fine; I'm tired. I think I'm just going to go to sleep." I rolled over, pulled up the covers, and turned my back to Don.

I woke up several times during the night to different hotel sounds. I looked over at Don, softly snoring, in the other bed. I kept trying to go back to sleep, but I couldn't. His phone was on the nightstand between us, so I quietly picked it up to check the number he had called earlier. It felt as if someone had punched me in the stomach, when I read *her* number on the phone—*nine* entries from earlier that day. *When did he have time to call her nine times? Is he really going to do this?* I lay there thinking I should pray, but I really couldn't think of what to pray for. I ended up praying for the guidance to handle what I needed to do with as much grace as possible.

The next morning, Don woke first, showered, and left to find some coffee. He grabbed his phone and said he would be back in a while. All the hope from yesterday that the situation would resolve itself when we returned home was gone. I realized the situation was out of my control. I decided to concentrate on the day at hand. I showered, dressed, and packed my overnight bag. I was ready to go when Don walked in with coffee.

When we arrived at Anna's dorm room, there seemed to be more parents than kids. The elevator was still utilized for moving in boxes, so the only option was the stairs. When we reached the eleventh floor and knocked on Anna's door, she greeted us in her robe.

"What are you doing here so early?" Anna mumbled.

Irritated, Don replied, "Anna, it's nine o'clock, and you knew we were coming to pick you up to open bank accounts today."

"My roommate is still asleep," Anna said in an argumentative tone.

"She isn't the one we need!" Don barked back, becoming increasingly more irritated.

I could see where the argument was going and knew we weren't going to accomplish anything standing in the hallway.

"Anna, your dad needs to return the trailer, and we need to take care of the dogs; just throw your hair in a ponytail and put on some clothes. We won't be gone that long. By the time we get back, Stacy will be up, and we can finish up any last-minute shopping you need to do," I negotiated.

"No, Mom, I'm not going out looking like this! You and Dad can just go eat breakfast and come back in an hour. I'll be ready then," Anna said petulantly.

"Anna, this place is going to be a zoo in an hour, and I don't want to fight my way back up eleven flights of stairs, *again*, in an hour. You can meet us in parking lot B over by the admissions building in one hour," I demanded.

"I can't get dressed and be over there in an hour!" Anna said, exasperated.

Don was ready to come unglued and shouted, *"Anna, you're being ridiculous!"*

I put my hand on Don's arm to stop the escalation and said, "Anna, we will meet you in an hour and fifteen minutes in parking lot B." She could tell by my tone that was the final offer and agreed.

An hour and fifteen minutes later, we met Anna in parking lot B and finished up last-minute errands. After lunch, we dropped her back on campus and said our good-byes. Don gave her a hug and last-minute instructions about her allowance and staying out of trouble. I was suddenly overcome with emotion. Between dealing with all the crushing humiliation and betrayal of Don's affair, and the feeling that someone was ripping my baby from my arms, all the feelings were coming fast and strong, as if a huge wave was about to knock me over. It felt as if I was about to lose everything. I was blinking back tears and feeling a crushing sense of panic, but that wasn't how I wanted to say good-bye. I just kept focusing on how infuriating she had been earlier, when she ordered us back down eleven flights of stairs to come back in an hour, to stop the flow of emotion that was about to overcome me.

I gave her a long hug and told her, "It's a good thing you are being such a pain-in-the-ass today, because it makes it easier to say good-bye."

We both laughed with tears in our eyes. I watched her walk toward her dorm as we pulled out of the parking lot and headed for home.

CHAPTER 3

On the way home, I was just plain mad. I was mad as hell at Don. I wanted to scream at that holier-than-thou bitch, Carol. I was mad at Ellen and my family for knowing all that time and not saying a word to me. I was mad at the Stones for bringing up the whole divorce statistics at dinner. I was mad at the dogs for every shoe, shrub, tool, and even back-porch railing that they had ever chewed. I was mad at school for starting in ten days. I couldn't even imagine how I was going to face a classroom of new students and put on that happy face to begin a new school year. *Ahhhhhhhhh!* Things were spiraling out of control. I hated everyone and everything at that point. For the next three hours, I just shut my eyes and pretended I was asleep. Don could just deal with the rest of the ride alone.

As we pulled into the drive, the dogs were joyfully running toward us. It's funny how dogs can sense when something is wrong. Normally, Jack would be jumping all over me, unable to contain his excitement, but that day, he sensed I was upset and stood next to me licking my hand. That one act of kindness from Jack was my undoing; the wave of emotion I had been holding back came flooding over me. It's easier to maintain control when you're mad at everyone. Jack just looked at me with questioning eyes. *Where is Anna? Why are you upset? Can I have a treat?*

Don was taking the U-Haul trailer off the car and attaching it to his little work truck, so we could pull the car into the garage.

He was going to head back into town, in his truck, to return the U-Haul to the rental company. After I gave the dogs a treat, Don asked me, "What are we going to do about Sunday dinner tomorrow?"

I didn't answer him. I just looked at him and thought, *Don't even fucking talk to me*, and walked into the house. I set my purse on the kitchen counter next to some green beans my father-in-law, Roger, must have picked. I carried my bag to my closet, shut the closet door, and collapsed on the floor and cried.

* * *

The next few weeks were a blur of activity. Setting up my classroom and beginning a new school year was oftentimes like launching a new play. The scenery had to be put in place. The characters had to learn all their lines and roles, and the show took massive amounts of preparation before it could begin. By the time I had my posters on the walls, the desks arranged, organized mountains of books, prepared lesson plans, and created fun activities for the first day, it was time to sit through endless meetings about the new reading program. The first month of school was exhausting; it often felt as if you were running with twenty-five kids in your arms, until they learned the routines and were able to run on their own.

* * *

We had made excuses to our parents why we couldn't host Sunday dinner for the last two weeks. I had tried to talk sense into Don over the affair, but he wasn't budging on his feelings toward his soul mate. One Friday evening, Mary, his mother, called and was wondering about Sunday dinner. I didn't have the energy to think of any more excuses. I knew if anyone could talk to Don, it would be her. I made the gut-wrenching decision to tell her about Don. I knew deep down that meant admitting final defeat.

"Mary, I need to tell you the truth; Don's been having an affair for the last year, and he wants a divorce."

"*What? You tell him to call me when he gets home!*" she said, appalled. We talked, briefly, about the situation. I could hear the shock and anger in her voice. I could also hear the confidence of a mother ready to reprimand her child and force him to correct the situation. After talking to Mary, I had a glimmer of hope that she could reason with Don.

When Don came home from work an hour later, I said, "Your mom called about Sunday dinner, and I told her the truth. She said for you to call her as soon as you were home."

He didn't say anything; he just picked up the phone and called them. I could hear him say, "Okay," as if someone had just died.

He hung up the phone and said dully, "I'm going over to my parents' house; I'll be home later." I tried to wait up for him, but by the time he came home I was already asleep in bed.

The next morning, Roger and Mary called. "Hi, Diane, are you going to be home this morning?"

I answered hesitantly, "Yes."

"Roger and I would like to come out and talk to you. We talked to Don last night, and we would really like to sit down and discuss this with you."

I tried to sound cheerful, and said, "Sure, come on out. I'll be here all day."

They were there fifteen minutes later. I could see in Mary's eyes that she had been crying. I had no idea what they were about to say. But the next words Mary spoke sentenced my marriage to death.

"Diane, you might as well agree to a divorce; he isn't going to let this woman go. I don't even know who he is. We talked to him for three hours straight last night, and I know when he has made up his mind like that, there is no changing it," Mary said with resigned conviction and inconsolable tears.

Tears were streaming down my face. Words wouldn't come; I just looked at her. I knew then it was over. She was my last hope. I knew what she said was the truth. It was as hard for her to tell me, as it was for me to hear. I could see the trepidation in their eyes; they were at a loss. For the longest time, we all just sat there while Mary and I cried.

Roger blew his nose and said, "I just want you to know; we are going to do what we can to hold Don accountable for his actions." Then he headed out to his garden.

Their kindness to me was overwhelming. Through my tears, I said, "This is all so humiliating. I want you to know how much I appreciate you and your support; it's just so humiliating to need it."

Telling my family was much easier. Ellen basically told them that I knew, and that was it. She thought I was "killing the messenger" because I had such limited discussions with them. I acknowledged my family was in an awkward position. I was glad Ellen had told me; her timing was the hurdle I had trouble getting over.

*   *   *

By September, life was settling into a routine at school. Anna had called several times, and she seemed happy. Her classes had started, and it appeared she was attending them regularly, in spite of her rushing a sorority, and parties in the dorm. I had the feeling the roommate situation wasn't working out, based on insinuations she was making about how many Chicago friends her roommate was entertaining. I didn't see her joining a sorority, either, but I thought the experience was good for her. Don was still living at home and sharing my bed. It was awkward, and everything seemed to be in a state of limbo, until one day when Ellen called.

I answered the phone, "Hey, Ellen."

"What are ya doin'?" asked Ellen.

"Just cleaning out some drawers. What's up?" I replied guardedly.

"Well, are you going to kill the messenger if I tell you the latest and greatest?" Ellen asked apologetically.

"No, what is it?" I asked warily.

"Okay, I'll tell you, but you can't get mad at me again," she admonished.

"I'm not; just say it!" I replied curtly.

"Well," Ellen sighed, "my neighbor, Kathleen Wells, said Don and Carol went to a special-education dinner together, and when Kathleen saw them, she went over to say hi. I guess Carol introduced him as her friend. Kathleen was stunned that Don was going along with the introduction, as if he hadn't known her for the last fifteen years while your kids all played sports together. She said it was as if he'd taken on another persona. She just left here, 'cause she came over to find out if you guys were divorced. I told her that I didn't know what was going to happen yet, but that Don *was* having an affair. Well, are you mad at me for saying that?" Ellen huffed.

I was stunned. *He is openly dating her in front of our friends and coming home and sleeping in our bed.* I tried to form a coherent reply when I said, "No, I'm not mad at you. When was this dinner?"

"Tonight," Ellen replied, like I hadn't been listening. "Is he there? Is he home yet? Are you going to say something to him? You need to throw his ass out!"

"No, he's not home yet. What else have you heard?" I asked slowly.

"Well, I can tell you; everybody is talking about it," she drawled.

I lied and said, "Hey, Anna is calling on the other line; I'll talk to you later." I hung up the phone, stared out over the pond, and prayed for guidance.

When Don came home, later, I calmly asked, "Did you enjoy the special-education lecture after your dinner tonight?" He froze, expecting a fight. I spoke in a monotone voice, "You have one week to move out," and then I walked upstairs and slept in Anna's room.

The next day, I went through the house like a mad woman. I had made up my mind I was going to surround myself with things and people I loved and get rid of anything that was even questionable.

Two days later, Don had a truck filled with every worthless piece of junk I could think, or want, to get rid of from the house. I laughed out loud at the sight of him pulling out of the drive. It was like a scene from *The Beverly Hillbillies*. The next thing to do was tell Anna. I told him that he was going to call her, in front of me, and we would tell her together. That night, I changed my mind and called Anna to prepare her for Don's call. As painful as I expected the call to be, she already knew. She was, of course, upset to hear the certainty of it from me.

We cried, and she asked, "Mom, do you want me to come home?"

I assured her, "No, Anna, what I need from you is to stay there, concentrate on good grades, and earn your degree. I want you to enjoy your college experience and try not to let this affect you. Your dad and I will work this out."

She shared stories from the past year that her friends had told her about Don and Carol, which they had heard from their parents. She had even confronted Don with the affair, after one of her teachers had asked her if we were divorced. She told Don she had heard he had been having an affair, and he had sworn there was nothing to the rumors. That was the part she was most upset about—he had lied to her face.

*   *   *

Up until that day, I had been avoiding almost everyone and concentrating on my classroom. I had made an appointment to consult a lawyer that Don had recommended. My appointment was scheduled for September 11, 2001, at 9:00 a.m. I was waiting, impatiently, in the lawyer's outer office when I noticed the names of the attorneys in the practice. Don had actually sent me to the law firm of Carol's brother. I was planning my exit strategy when the attorney I had an appointment with stepped out from his office apologizing for the delay. We sat down in his office, but before he could say a word, I recited my excuse about a conflict of interest. I explained that the woman my husband was having an affair with was his law partner's sister. He looked extremely sympathetic and referred me to another divorce attorney's office. The anxiety of having to find another attorney, compounded with the reality I was moving forward toward a divorce, left me feeling as if my world was collapsing.

I had taken the morning off and had to be back at work at eleven thirty. It was only ten, so I decided to stop by my friend Lisa's house. She knew I was anxious about the appointment with the attorney and had told me to come over for lunch if I had time. She answered the door visibly upset. I thought it was for my benefit, but I learned, very quickly, as we watched the replays of the Twin Towers coming down in New York, that it wasn't just my world collapsing that day. By ten thirty, we were beginning to process the devastating images on the TV when another plane crash was announced at the Pentagon. By that point, her mom and husband had called. Tears were silently streaming down my face at the horror on TV. I truly questioned whether the world was coming to an end that day. Lisa and I were praying together, out of fear, when the next plane crash was reported in Pennsylvania. It was around eleven then, and I had to compose myself, because I was due back at school in thirty minutes. I felt the entire world was falling apart. *My* overwhelming grief was camouflaged by our nation's grief. The whole country was terrified.

When I walked into school at eleven thirty, I didn't have to explain where I had been or why I was upset. The entire school was panicked by the devastation and was deliberating whether we should close school. Mass evacuations were under way in DC and New York. Americans felt benevolence toward one another that day and longed for the comfort of family and loved ones. Parents came to school to take their children home, and the secretary didn't ask for an excuse.

When I came home from school that day, I called Anna; she said her dad had called earlier. We talked about nothing and everything as we watched replays from the terrorist attacks. Her roommate's father had been in Minnesota on business and was on his way home when his plane was diverted to Canada, because all planes had been grounded. We created a plan for her to come home in the event that the terror escalated and school closed.

When it was time to hang up, I said, "I love you, baby, just call, and I'll drive down if something happens, and you need to come home."

"I love you too, Mom. I hate thinking that you are out in the country alone," Anna cried.

"I'm not alone, honey, I have these damn dogs." I tried to laugh, but my voice was cracking, and I was wiping a stream of silent tears. "I'll be fine; let's be positive and focus on what needs to be done. You have school, and I have work. We need to focus on the positives right now, or we'll just drive ourselves crazy."

"Okay, mom. I'll call you tomorrow," Anna said, trying to choke back a sob.

"Okay, bye," I said before I broke into sobs. Even though my heart was breaking when we hung up, I was so grateful to still have her to hold and talk to, unlike thousands of 9/11 victims. Whining over my divorce seemed petty and trivial in light of 9/11. I watched the replays of people in the midst of debris running through streets and walking over bridges like zombies. I witnessed *real* tragedy and listened to devastating stories play out each day in the news. I was thankful my biggest problem was the divorce. It was time to put on my big girl panties and deal with building *my* life again. I knew I should be grateful to have a life to rebuild. I vowed to myself I was going to pull it together and only look forward, unless I could learn something from looking back.

CHAPTER 4

The next months were consumed with the events of 9/11, school, sorting through twenty-three years of memories, collaborating with divorce attorneys, and fielding phone calls from different people offering me their support. I was actually surprised how little I missed Don. I realized that with Anna gone, he played little to no role in my life. He had distanced himself from me long ago; I just had been too busy to notice. At first, my anger staved off any fear of staying alone in the country at night. Jack, Jill, and my alarm system also kept a wall of defense from the fear, but not from the loneliness. I still saw Don frequently, as I had stipulated in the separation papers that he had to mow, plow snow, and buy the fifty-pound bags of dog food.

We were able to maintain civility, with the exception of one afternoon when Don was at the house. He had finished weed-eating around the pond, filled two plastic cans in the garage with fifty-pound bags of dog food, and hauled several heavy bags of salt down to the water softener in the basement. We were standing in the kitchen bantering over something trivial, when his next words stopped every thought and muscle in my body and replaced it with white-hot rage.

Dripping with condescension, he said, "You need to get a life."

I threw my arm in the air to flip him off, and by accident, I swear, my hand caught his temple. Almost by reflex, and before I had any control of my thoughts, my other fist came at him from the other hand, and before I knew it, I was beating the shit out of him while he was covering his head with his arms from my blows.

I was screaming, "You son of a bitch! I had a life! I gave it to you for the last twenty-three years, and *you trashed it!*" When I was too tired to throw one more punch, my foot entered the fight with one swift kick to his balls; after that, it was all over. He was holding himself on his knees when I said, "Don't. Ever. Talk. To. Me. That. Way. Again!"

That afternoon was extremely cathartic. I was tired of carrying around so much anger—anger toward Don, the divorce, 9/11, and all my other irritations. I felt like I had opened a door that I had been struggling to keep closed and released all my anger. It was a moment of clarity. I took my power back. I wasn't taking his, or any other man's, bullshit anymore.

*   *   *

One evening later that week, I had a call from Randy Gonz. I had known Randy for more than twenty years along with his wife, Cindy. I had gone to high school with Cindy and later worked with her at my first job after college. We had babies at the same time, shared play dates with the girls, and, occasionally, enjoyed dinner in each other's home. When Randy called, I felt an immediate sense of panic that something had happened to Cindy, as it was peculiar that Randy would call. I used to evade conversations with Randy; he would make vague comments that bordered on inappropriate. It was subtle; there was a double entendre so that he could plead innocent if I appeared offended. They had moved out of state, and we had lost touch with them over the years.

"Hello," I answered.

"Hi, Diane, this is Randy Gonz. How are you doing?" he asked, but it felt like a solicitation.

"Fine." I hesitated and then asked, "Everything okay with Cindy?"

"Oh, yeah, the girls are fine. I was in town for the weekend, and I thought I'd call and say hey," he replied, with the veiled implication he wanted to do more than say hey.

"Is Cindy with you? It's been too long since we've done lunch and shopping together," I answered, leaving no ambiguity to the pompous ass that I only had interest in getting together with Cindy.

"No, but *I'd* take you up on lunch," he said.

"I really can't, but have Cindy call me," I subtly warned. Oddly, enough, she didn't call.

Randy was under the mistaken impression women going through divorces were horny and waiting for his phone call. It was demeaning and insulting. I had already made up my mind that I would not allow any man to speak to me in a degrading manor ever again.

*   *   *

Most of my married women friends acted like I had a contagious disease. I realized, then, I had probably offended most of my divorced friends. I had the misconception that I had been supportive when I'd bashed their ex-husbands, but in reality, I just made them feel more insecure. Or worse, I ignored their pain by distancing myself from them. I wanted to rectify any wounds I may have caused them. I sent out a mass e-mail to old friends updating them on my marital situation. I acknowledged that divorce was awkward for everyone and that words people say are not as important as the intentions behind them. I was truly sorry if I had not been a supportive friend to those who had experienced a divorce. I hadn't understood the devastation of divorce.

After that, it was like floodgates had opened, and I received e-mails from people I hadn't talked to in years. I enjoyed coming home from work and reading all my new e-mails that had been generated from my original update. I had begun writing regular updates when I realized it was easier to keep my family and friends informed and do rumor control at the same time.

Ellen had forwarded my updates to a friend of hers, Marie. Marie had asked her if I was interested in meeting a friend of hers that was going through a similar situation. I told Ellen, "Sure, give her my e-mail address and tell her to e-mail me."

*   *   *

A few days later, I was reading e-mails when an instant message popped up from the username Aviator, "Marie's friend, Mick." I was surprised Maria's friend was male.

> **Aviator:** Hello, Diane, this is Marie's friend, Mick Ashmore. Are you there?

I thought about whether to respond and typed back:

> **Teach5:** Yes, I'm here, how are you?
> **Aviator:** So what are you wearing? Just kidding!! Trying to make this less awkward lol.
> **Teach5:** lol, I hear you are going through a divorce too.
> **Aviator:** wife left with friend that we'd just returned from Tahiti with, and I was paying him to give her flying lessons!
> **Teach5:** Mine found his soul mate with the superintendent's wife, only he died so they figured they were meant to be.
> **Aviator:** My fingers are too big for these keys; it is taking me too long to impress you with my typing skills since I do more correcting than typing, would it be ok if I called you?

Maybe it was the anonymity of it all, but his reference to big hands elicited an instant, playful response.

> **Teach5:** So do you have big feet too? lol
> **Aviator:** As a matter of fact I do . . . can I call you?

I let out a giggle, intrigued by the banter between us. *Why shouldn't he call me; I'm separated.* I was wrestling with what to say next . . .

Teach5: Sure

Aviator: Is now ok to call you what is your number

Teach5: 555-820-2436.

Mick called one minute later, and we talked for two hours about everything from our kids to our impending divorce proceedings. He was a hospital administrator in town. It seemed to be a very stressful job; he had to make many ethical decisions balancing patient care with profits. He had a pilot's license and owned an airplane. We shared many personal feelings and stories; it was like free therapy.

*   *   *

Initially, after Don left, I felt socially inept. I didn't know how to function alone. After a while, I began to realize I could do whatever I wanted. It was *my* decision to watch whatever *I* wanted on TV, eat when *I* wanted and what *I* wanted, stay up all night and read, luxuriate in a hot bath whenever I wanted, or go to a movie *I* wanted to see. The grocery store was a whole new, liberating experience. I bought the cookies *I* liked. I no longer shopped with a cart; instead, I chose a hand basket and tried foods I had never tasted. Instead of a full meat-and-potato-type meal, I learned I had more energy from a diet of nuts, fruits, and vegetables. I found I had a completely different flavor palate than what I had been cooking all those years.

CHAPTER 5

The months of stress were a great weight-loss plan. I was too thin for my clothes. I was between a size 2 and a 4, whereas I used to be between a 6 and an 8. My baggy teacher-clothes hung off my shoulders and sagged off my hips. I resembled a bag lady, until the day I walked into Talbots and met Cheryl Busing. Cheryl was about my height, age, and build, happily divorced for the last three years, and loved fashion, drinking, and gossip. She zeroed in on me the minute I stepped in the door.

"Hi, I'm Cheryl. You're Diane, aren't you?" she asked, as if she had been expecting me.

"I am . . . I'm sorry, have we met before?" I was trying to run through a list of past students' parents that she might be.

"No, not officially; we have mutual friends, and I've always heard such nice things about you," she replied confidently.

I realized that when your husband has had a year long affair with the county superintendent's wife, that the entire county is gossiping about the juicy details of the widow's escapes, and, by default, I reached small-town celebrity status as the jilted wife in the scandal. It was difficult to avoid the sympathetic expressions from nearly everyone. Cheryl's acquaintance was devoid of the condescending tones that I tolerated from others. She presented herself as a comrade.

Cheryl read my inner dialogue and, effortlessly, transitioned the conversation back to shopping.

"Are you looking for anything in particular today?" she asked as she gave my outfit a concerned look.

"Well, I've lost some weight lately, and I need to pick up a few things that fit," I answered carefully.

Cheryl started pulling clothes from racks and shelves and coordinating accessories. Initially, I thought all the sizes would be too small or too tight, but quickly realized she knew exactly what she was doing. I went from frumpy to fabulous in one afternoon.

Two hours later, Cheryl and I knew each other's whole life histories. I walked out of Talbots with a new wardrobe and a late lunch date with her in an hour, when she would be finished for the day. The lunch date turned into happy hour and then dinner. We talked and laughed for hours; it turned out that Cheryl's ex-husband, Tom, was the attorney that I had visited on 9/11. That day he had been so distraught by the bombing of the Twin Towers that he had driven over to her house, after I left, to be near his kids. He confessed to her how his law partner had choreographed a divorce consultation with him that morning for his sister, Carol, so that they could keep tabs on how the divorce was proceeding. The plan was to refer me to one of their friends, if I had realized it was the law firm where her brother worked. But, after the bombing, and meeting me, Tom had a change of heart and referred me to the best divorce attorney he knew. He had told her that, in light of the day's events, he didn't want their scheming on his conscience, too.

I was in such high spirits when I drove home. It had been so long since I felt so joyful. When I pulled into the drive, the dogs followed me up to the garage. Jack dropped a stick at my feet and then sprinted into the yard turning in circles before he plopped down on his belly, ready to pounce as soon as I threw the stick. Jill relaxed on the back porch and seemed to enjoy watching the gaiety of the game. I picked up the stick and threw it in the air, along with my worries.

*   *   *

Later, after the dogs were put up for the night, I was hanging the new clothes in my closet when Anna called. She decided sorority life wasn't for her; she didn't like being told what to wear or have her schedule filled with silly activities. Her grades were good. She said she would be catching a ride home for Thanksgiving break the following Tuesday, with Becky's parents, sometime between 4:00 and 6:00 p.m. We discussed different scenarios of how we thought Don would fit into the break. She was pretty mad at him. We were going to Ellen's house for Thanksgiving dinner. Ellen had invited Roger and Mary, since they had always shared holiday dinners with my family. Mary was still undecided whether they would come, but my parents were encouraging them and had offered to drive down with them. There were usually between forty to fifty family members who attend our Thanksgiving dinners so, it was easy to blend in at Ellen's. A huge buffet of food is laid along the kitchen's center island and countertops. Seating choices include the formal dining room, which seats twenty-six, or the bar area, which easily accommodates thirty at the various tables and bar. Traditionally, the older relatives sit in the dining room, while little kids and their parents choose the bar area.

We talked for close to an hour before we agreed we weren't going to stress out over break. She was anxious to see my new wardrobe and sleep in her own bed. I couldn't wait to see her; it would be so comforting to have someone else in the house at night.

*   *   *

Around four the following Tuesday evening, I heard the dogs barking and looked out to see the Stones pulling in the drive with Anna. I ran outside to keep the dogs from jumping on their car. Jack had grabbed one of Anna's bags in his mouth and was flinging it back and forth like a rag doll, while Jill was nuzzling Anna's hand for attention.

I laughed, thanked the Stones for bringing her home, and said, "Welcome home." The Stones were in a hurry to put distance from our dogs, when they said, "We'll call you about the ride home," and pulled out of the drive.

Anna laughed and squealed, "Get that bag from Jack; it's got all my makeup!"

I tried wrestling the bag from Jack, but between being so excited to see Anna and fully enjoying the game of tug-of-war, he wasn't about to let go of the bag. I could see him eyeing her other bags.

"Anna, grab your other bags before he lifts his leg!" I yelled.

Anna grabbed her bags just in time. Jill took a bite at Jack's tail; she knew his tricks.

"Anna, throw your bags inside and grab some dog treats. Maybe Jack will trade your bag for a treat," I suggested.

Anna gave Jill a treat and then tried negotiating for her bag from Jack with the other one.

"Jack, you wanna treat?" Anna coaxed.

He didn't. I hated to do it, but I had to pull out the big guns—the all-day chew bones. These were usually reserved for when we would be gone for the whole day. As soon as I reached into the upper garage cabinet, Jack's ears perked up with anticipation. He carried her bag into the garage. If I didn't want to sit down and visit with Anna so badly, I would never have given him that eight-dollar bone, and, of course, Jill, too.

"Jack, drop it!" I demanded, holding the chew bones.

Jill immediately sat down politely. Jack dropped the drool-covered bag onto the concrete floor, where Anna quickly grabbed it. I gave the dogs their undeserved bones, and they trotted happily to the backyard while Anna and I went inside and carried her bags upstairs to unpack.

As we dropped her bags in her closet, she twirled around and squealed, "Oh, my closet, I've missed you!"

I laughed. It was such a relief to have her home and hear her laughing. We talked as she unpacked and made plans for dinner. She had been craving LaGondola spaghetti, so we decided to run into town and bring it back to the house. Later, we watched TV in her room and talked and cried late into the night. I fell asleep in her bed that night; it was so consoling to share a bed and have someone else in the house.

The next morning, I quietly went downstairs to let the dogs out and put on a pot of coffee. Ellen called and asked if Anna would be up for babysitting, so that she could prepare for Thanksgiving Day. Ellen was very generous with Anna. I knew she would probably pay Anna a hundred dollars for an afternoon of babysitting. It was her way of giving Anna "pocket money" for college. I couldn't imagine Anna would turn her down, and I suggested she bring the kids to our house, since she had to come into town for groceries anyway. They lived in Riva, a small town on the opposite side of Springfield from where we lived. We agreed she'd bring the kids to my house around ten o'clock, and I'd drop them back at their house around five o'clock.

Later, I heard Anna upstairs on her cell phone; from what I could hear, it sounded as if she was talking to Don.

When she came downstairs, I said, "Hey, Ellen called and asked if she brought the kids over for the day, if you'd babysit?"

"Yeah, you told her that I would, right?" Anna asked enthusiastically.

"I did; she is going to bring them here around ten, and I'll take them back around five. You can come with me if you want," I replied.

Anna tentatively answered, "Actually, that would be good if you drop them off, because Dad called and wants to have dinner with me around six tonight." She looked at me, gauging my reaction.

"Okay, that sounds good. It'll give me the opportunity to help Ellen with last-minute details and visit for a while, after I drop off the kids." I sensed her relief at my response.

Later, after I returned home from dropping off the kids, I made a dessert to take to Ellen's the next day. Anna was still out with her dad, and I was mulling over what Ellen had said earlier, about them moving. Her husband, Keith, was being transferred to somewhere on the Gulf Coast. They were still deciding if Keith should rent an apartment until the kids were out of school, and they had a chance to sell the house.

Later, Anna walked into the kitchen after putting the dogs up for the night.

"How was dinner?" I asked cheerfully.

"Weird," Anna sulked. "Dad kept saying he was sorry all night, but I know he doesn't mean it. I don't want to think about it anymore. It's been a long night just trying to have a conversation with him. We don't have anything to talk about, as long as he is with that woman."

I decided to switch gears, so I wouldn't start ripping on her dad.

"Well, I heard some news today. Ellen and Keith are moving to the Gulf Coast," I said with a sigh.

"What, are you kidding?" Anna huffed, aggravated. "When are they moving?"

"It won't be for a while," I said. "They have loads of details to work out before they actually move. Keith will probably go first, and then Ellen and the kids will go down when the kids are out of school."

Before she could answer, Anna's phone rang; it was Shelby.

"Mom, do you care if some friends come over?" Anna asked.

"No, that's fine; just don't eat this dessert, it's for dinner tomorrow," I replied firmly.

With Anna home, and kids running in and out of the house, it was if nothing had ever changed. I stayed up and visited for a while, but after they put in a movie I didn't want to watch, I pleaded exhaustion and went to bed.

The next day at Thanksgiving dinner, I was glad to see Roger and Mary. They had decided to drive down alone, instead of riding with my parents. I figured they wanted their own car there, in case dinner was awkward. As it turned out, they enjoyed themselves and were some of the last to leave. The dinner conversation evolved around Ellen's move, Anna's school, and the latest events of the grandchildren. Any apprehension I had that my divorce would make the day awkward was laid to rest.

CHAPTER 6

I decided to check my e-mail, after dropping Anna and Becky at the train station. They had decided to take the train back to SIU after Thanksgiving break with their Chicago friends, who were reserving seats for them. I was happy to pay for their tickets to save myself the six-hour drive there and back. I was feeling depressed and sorry for myself, when the computer dinged, and an IM box popped up.

> **Aviator:** So what are you wearing?

I laughed, as that had become his opening line after his initial contact with me. I decided to continue the repartee.

> **Teach5:** Not a thing, just lying here waiting for you to call
> **Aviator:** You do know this is Mick don't you?

I laughed even harder then and typed:

> **Teach5:** Yes, I know it's you I WAS KIDDING!!
> **Aviator:** You shouldn't say things like that to a man who has not had sex in a very long time

I thought, *Whoa! I guess I started this, didn't I?*

> **Teach5:** How long has it been?
> **Aviator:** too long, why? are you interested?

I was wondering what he looked like. We had probably accumulated over twenty-five hours talking on the phone over the past months. I felt as if I knew him pretty well. *I'd be up for a* one-night stand with him. I deserved it. I'd never done anything like that in my life. I guess, technically, it wouldn't be a one-night stand since we knew each other, although we hadn't formally met.

Teach5: our lives are pretty complicated right now
Aviator: You didn't answer my question.
Teach5: lol

*   *   *

A few weeks before Anna was due home for Christmas break, Ellen called and asked if I'd go ice-skating with her and the kids. She couldn't manage them alone on the ice. It was Saturday, and I didn't have any plans, so I agreed to meet her for the noon skate at the indoor ice rink at the Civic Center. I was skating around with my six-year-old niece when a good-looking man flew past me on hockey skates, checking me out with a long head-to-toe look. I watched him make the corner, gracefully leaning in, with one leg crossing the other. He was older than me; with some gray at the temples, an athletic build and a Robert Redford look about him. I was instantly attracted to him and looked around only to find he had left the ice. I bribed my niece with the promise of a hot pretzel from the refreshment stand so that she would leave the ice with me for a second look at him. By the time we left the ice, he was gone. I was pleasantly surprised at myself that I had noticed a good-looking man. *It must be the flirty chat with Mick that has given me the confidence to start thinking about meeting new men.*

*   *   *

I became aware of the attention I had received from men since Don left. I had worn my mommy/teacher clothes like a label for years. After losing weight, I had a teenager's figure again and, thanks to Cheryl, a new tight-fitting wardrobe. I started noticing a different reception from people. I could tell some of my friends were not comfortable with the change. I had the impression I was being judged because of my new look. I lightened my hair a few shades closer to the color of my teens, and I had extra time to have my nails done regularly. My new look opened doors to places I hadn't been in years. Men were asking me for help at the grocery store, were holding doors open, were giving me quicker service, and were actually *interested* in me, rather than just answering me.

*   *   *

After I had returned home from the skating rink, I was upstairs looking for something to watch on TV when the doorbell rang. I looked out the window and saw Jack in the back of a truck. I answered the front door and was met by a tall, muscular, good-looking man holding Jack's collar.

"Hi, I'm John Nichols. I have the farm down the road. Your dog was chasing a deer and ran through his fence," he said, handing me Jack's shock collar.

I gave Jack a reprimanding look, and he smiled back, saying, "See what I brought you?"

As I took the collar from John, I said, "Thanks for bringing him back. I'm Diane." I could hardly keep my smile to a minimum; he was so cute. We were standing there staring at each other, until he turned toward the truck, and I followed him. I reached up to put Jack's collar back on, and by then, Jill was jumping at the truck.

John took the collar back, and said, "Here let me help you with that," as he buckled the collar around Jack.

"Jill, down," I said futilely. "I'm sorry; these dogs aren't very well behaved."

John opened the tailgate, and Jack pounced on Jill. They started running in circles and nipping at each other's tails. Jack was so happy to be home and pestering Jill that he ignored us and ran to the back chasing Jill.

"They're good-looking dogs," John said, trying to extend the conversation.

"Thanks. So . . . you have the farm with the horses that back up to my pasture?" I asked, not wanting our meeting to end, either. I noticed he didn't wear a wedding ring. He was about my age, wore cowboy boots, worn jeans, and a brown Carhartt jacket. He had loose brown curls, falling out of his cowboy hat and over his ears. He removed his aviator sunglasses to reveal soulful hazel eyes.

"Well, horses are a part of the farm. I've raised Clydesdales for Anheuser Busch for years, and I have a few painted and palominos to ride. I might be selling the painted, though; they were for my ex, and she isn't riding them regularly, now. I don't have time to ride them and take care of the farm. As much as I hate to say it, I think they're going to be sold."

"Oh, that's a shame," I said, happy to hear the "ex."

"Yeah. Do you ride?"

"Not well, but I'd like to learn," I said eagerly. "Do you have kids that ride?" I asked, fishing.

"My kids are grown and married. One lives in Florida, and the other is in Louisiana. They used to show horses and cows when they were little, but they've got their own lives now. What about you?" He asked, pushing back his hat.

"I have one daughter in college and a soon-to-be ex. Right now, I'm living here by myself, although I don't want to advertise that," I said, questioning whether I should have told him.

"No offense, but pretty much everybody knows. I was in the same situation a few years ago, so I know what you are going through. Just keep looking forward, and you'll get through it okay. If it makes you feel any safer, most of us along this road keep an eye out for you."

"That's comforting to know. I should have guessed everyone knew," I said, a little embarrassed.

"Well, I think your ex is an idiot. You should ride with me sometime."

"I'd love to. Are your horses gentle? I'm really a novice," I said, feeling inept on so many levels.

"What's your number? I'll call you, when I get a chance to ride. Or . . . you're welcome to come down and acquaint yourself with them before we ride if you like."

"Okay, that sounds like fun."

I gave him my number, and he said he would call me. I thanked him for bringing Jack back and went back inside, smiling all the way.

*   *   *

The following Thursday, I had just returned from a Christmas party with the teachers from school and was putting the dogs in for the night, when the phone rang. I raced inside to answer it, hoping it was John.

"Hello."

A man's voice whispered into the phone, "What are you wearing?"

"Hi, Mick," I laughed.

"What have you been up to lately?" he asked cheerfully.

"Nothing and everything; school is winding down for Christmas break, and, of course, Anna will be home next week, too. I need to decorate the house before she comes home so it feels like Christmas. What about you? What have you been up to?"

"I'm going to meet my son in Colorado and do some skiing over the Christmas holiday, so I've been working on that. I've been doing some ice-skating on my lunch hour to try and tone my leg muscles for skiing."

My stomach flipped at the thought that the guy I saw at the rink might be Mick.

I asked, "Were you ice-skating last Saturday at the Civic Center?"

"Yeah, I think I was."

"Did you have on khaki pants with a blue shirt and hockey skates?"

"I don't remember what I was wearing, but I do have hockey skates."

"I think I saw you there. I was there with my sister and her kids."

"I think I remember seeing a couple of women who looked like sisters with their kids. But then again, there were lots of kids there that day. I don't know what I was thinking going on a Saturday. I left after the first fifteen minutes, because it was too crowded. You should have said something; I've been thinking we should meet."

"Now you say that, since you saw me," I teased.

"I've wanted to meet you for a long time. I keep tabs on you through mutual friends; I knew you weren't ready," he said pedantically.

"Hmm, keeping tabs on me, huh?" I was, actually, very flattered and touched at such a thoughtful remark.

"Where would you want to meet?" I asked.

"I think we would both agree we don't need to fuel the rumor mills surrounding our divorces by meeting in a public place," he suggested.

"That's true. You could come over here *tomorrow* night. But I have to warn you, *Grey's Anatomy* begins at eight, and you can only talk during commercials."

Mick laughed and said, "Well, how about if I pick up some dinner and come around seven o'clock? Then, if you don't like me, you can get rid of me before your show starts."

I laughed and said, "That sounds like a good idea."

The next day at school, I had a hard time focusing on anything but the clock. By the time three o'clock rolled around, I was all but tossing the last student out of my room so I could leave.

I showered, shaved my legs, painted my toenails, and put on my lotion and perfume. *What am I doing?*

Mick pulled in the drive at seven o'clock sharp. I had put the dogs up, until he was in the house. I answered the front door and invited him to come in. He was tall, good-looking with green eyes, and had blondish hair with salt and pepper at the temples.

"This is for you," he said, handing me a little Christmas bag.

"Aww, that's so sweet. Thank you," I said nervously, thinking, *he does have big hands . . . and big feet!*

I wasn't expecting the gift at all.

"Can I take your coat?" He wore a long, gray, cashmere topcoat, a light blue dress shirt, and navy dress slacks. He smelled like Polo Sport.

He slipped the bag of Chinese food from his arm and casually shrugged out of his coat before handing it to me.

"Where do we want this?" he asked as he held up the Chinese food.

"Let's take it into the kitchen," I said, trying to appear casual.

We sat at the kitchen island, instead of the table, because I was trying to make our encounter as relaxed as possible.

"I need to let the dogs out; I'll be right back."

"I want to see the infamous Jack and Jill. I've heard so much about them," Mick said, amused.

"Okay, you know what you are in for," I warned.

We walked out to the garage, and Jack started jumping on me immediately.

Mick said in a calm, patient voice, "Jack. Sit." He was holding the palm of his hand forward toward Jack. At first, I thought sarcastically, *Yeah, right, he's going to sit.* Then, Jack sat! Mick rubbed his ears and said "Good boy." He looked at me and said, "These are good-tempered and intelligent dogs, what are you going to do with them if you sell the house?"

I was dumfounded. As I gave Jack the "stink-eye," I mumbled something about crossing that bridge when I came to it. I let the dogs out, and we returned to the kitchen.

I grabbed a couple of plates and could feel his perusing eyes scrutinizing me. He was unpacking the cartons and holding the fortune cookies.

"Should we read these now to see if we should continue our date?" he asked.

"Are we on a date?" I bantered. "I thought we were just meeting each other."

"Oh, no, dinner and a movie is a date," he teased.

"Well, technically, it's dinner and a TV show, and, remember, you can only talk during commercials," I teased.

"I promise, I'll be good," he said suggestively.

Okay, how well do I know this guy? I'm completely alone with this man in the country. Nobody knows he's here, and he suggesting he'll be good at a whole lot more than being quiet through Grey's Anatomy.

I tilted my head with a grin, raised one eyebrow, put my hand on my hip, and said in my stern teacher voice, "You don't wanta mess with *this* school teacher."

Mick laughed a deep belly laugh, as he held his hands up in surrender. We enjoyed our Moo goo gai pan, fried rice, and spring rolls together. He passed me a fortune cookie as he unwrapped his.

He read aloud, "Never regret. If it's good, it's wonderful. If it's bad, it's experience."

Mine read, "Get ready. Good fortune comes in bunches." I smiled as I thought about both Mick and John.

I cleared the dishes, and we went upstairs to watch *Grey's Anatomy* in the family room. It had the biggest TV and an oversized pit group that had seen years of use. As I became engrossed in the show, I unconsciously tucked my feet under Mick's legs for warmth. He was so easy to be around. It felt as if we were old friends. He had been married for twenty-six years; we were both used to the comfortable routines of a partner.

"I'm sorry," I said, pulling my feet back to my side.

He grabbed my feet and put them in his lap, winked at me, and mouthed, "I'm good with my hands." He acted as if he was locking his lips with an invisible key to remind me that he wasn't allowed to talk.

I laughed nervously and thought, *I bet you are.*

I could hardly concentrate on the show as he rubbed my feet. All I could think was *he is good with his hands.*

After the show, I said I needed to let the dogs back in, subtly indicating it was time for him to go. He was the perfect gentleman. He put on his coat, and I walked him to the door. He reached his arms around me to give me a hug and grabbed my butt with a quick squeeze.

"Cute butt," he said with a wink. He bent down and gave me a quick kiss on the lips. He had soft lips that sent a wake-up call all the way to my toes.

The quick exchange lasted all of three seconds, but the feelings he woke lingered long after he left. As I shut the door, I saw John's truck driving by very slowly. I ran to the side window and caught a glimpse of John checking out Mick. *Drag! Talk about poor timing . . .*

I felt as if I'd almost gotten away with something I wasn't supposed to do. As I turned around, I realized my Christmas gift from Mick was still sitting on the table. I had forgotten to open it. I reached in the bag and pulled out a red Aromatique Christmas candle. The card said, "I remember you saying this was your favorite potpourri, a little something to motivate your Christmas decorating."

He was so thoughtful. And funny. And good-looking. And smelled good. I e-mailed him later that night to thank him for the candle and dinner. I told him that I enjoyed meeting him, *on our first date*, and was reading my other e-mail, when my IM box dinged.

Aviator: You are quite welcome. I also enjoyed our date. I'm looking forward to our second date.

Yippee, he wants to go out again. Although, it really isn't going out, I guess.

Teach5: Me too. We'll have to plan something after the holidays when Anna goes back to school.

Aviator: I'll call you when I get back from Colorado around Jan 5th

Teach5: Okay have a great holiday if I don't talk to you

Aviator: You too

CHAPTER 7

Don had driven down to SIU and picked up the girls for Christmas break. Anna was home and upstairs on the computer, when she yelled downstairs.

"Mom, who is Aviator, and why does he want to know what I'm wearing?"

I chortled and yelled back, "It's a joke; he's a friend of mine. Let him know it's you and *not* me."

Anna walked downstairs, and said, shocked, "*He's?*"

I gave her a quick synopsis of his circumstances and told her that we were e-mailing. She wasn't about to let it end there. She plopped down on the couch next to me. "Have you talked to him?" she asked in disbelief.

"Yes, we've talked quite a bit actually. He's like free therapy." I tried to sound nonchalant.

"Have you met him?" she asked curiously.

"Just once, we met for Chinese food." I left out that we met here. *Why am I twisting this? I haven't done anything wrong.*

I tried to be as truthful as possible throughout the rest of the inquisition. She was a little stunned that I was talking to a man, but I sensed a genuine relief in her that I had met someone that I could relate to.

On Christmas Eve we went to the five o'clock Mass. It was awkward going to church and watching everyone avoid eye contact with us. Don had always coordinated ushers for Mass, so we were used to having good seats at Christmas Mass and being greeted warmly. It was as if the church felt betrayed, too. Those same people, who were always wanting favors and inviting us to participate in activities, suddenly didn't recognize me. We sat in the middle of a pew in the back surrounded by crying children. At a time in my life when I actually needed a church family, they not only turned their backs, but later also forbade me from receiving Communion once the divorce was final. *Church rules; not God's.*

After Mass, I dropped Anna at Roger and Mary's traditional Christmas Eve dinner, to which I was no longer invited. I realized it was awkward for everyone; I didn't hold it against them, but it still hurt. Later, Don dropped her back at the house.

Instead of the traditional early-morning Christmas gift exchange, we slept in late and had a leisurely breakfast. Later, we went to my brother's house, where everyone had gathered for a festive dinner and another gift exchange. I wondered what Don did.

Anna's friends were around most of the break. She had stayed close to home, as there was close to eight inches of snow on the ground, and her friends came out to ride the snowmobile around the fields and ice-skate on the pond.

Anna had made the dean's list at SIU and seemed to be interested in a new boy that was enrolled in law school there. I didn't give that much hope, as Anna needed way more attention than any law student could afford to give. I had been immersed in my classroom and divorce negotiations with Don prior to break, so it was comforting to relax and visit with the kids and family.

Becky's parents were driving the girls back to SIU. I was relieved that I didn't have to drive, so that I wouldn't have to drive back on the icy roads, alone.

*   *   *

One January evening, after Anna had gone back to school from Christmas break, I was grading papers, and out of the blue, an old friend, Jeanie Brady, called. Jeanie had gone back to school, at the local junior college, about five years ago, after her nasty divorce. At the time, I was taking a children's literature class at the same community college. We met in the parking lot, one day, when she had locked her keys in her car. She was upset and crying at having no success in breaking into her car with a coat hanger. I offered her a ride to her house to pick up an extra set of keys. We became very close friends for the duration of that semester. We would meet for coffee before our classes started, and she would tell the wildest tales of her marriage and family. She was high energy and made going back to school fun. Eventually, we lost touch over the years, when she transferred to a college out of town. Jeanie was like a squeaky cheerleader. Everything she said and did was exaggerated and magnified. She had a loud, shrill voice that didn't seem to match her tiny frame. She kept her long, waist-length hair from the '70s and wore her bangs pinned in a puffed '80s-style barrette. She loved to wear lots of makeup and dressed like a teenager.

"Hello," I answered cautiously, not recognizing the phone number on the caller ID.

"Hi, Diane, this is Jeanie Brady! How are you? I got your number from Cheryl Busing. She was telling me all about what an asshole Don turned out to be. I can't believe he left *you* for *her*. Cheryl told me that you are *way* cuter and that *she* is *way* older than Don. So how are you doing?"

Whoa, that was a lot from one hello, but I wouldn't expect less from Jeanie.

"I'm fine. I didn't know you knew Cheryl," I replied.

"Oh, yeah, we've known each other since high school; her husband took care of my divorce," gushed Jeanie. "She came in for Botox at the spa where I'm working. Whoops, I shouldn't say that, but she won't care, and you won't tell anyone. I'm working as a physician's assistant in Dr. Lee's med spa. You should come in, or, better yet, we should all get together and do skin peels at one of our houses."

"Okay," I lied. "That sounds like fun. Or maybe we could meet for drinks," I said, hoping for the second option.

"Great! What about meeting tomorrow night at Robbies around six thirty?" she asked.

I hadn't been to Robbies since I was separated. It was a small, narrow, pub-like restaurant that was a popular place for the forty-plus crowd. There was always an animated group of attractive single women hanging out together at the high tables at the end of the bar. I had always been one of the couples sitting at a small two-person table against the brick wall opposite the bar.

"Okay, that sounds like fun," I answered, looking forward to seeing her again.

"Perfect! I'll call Cheryl and see if she can meet too. First one there needs to grab a high table at the end of the bar, okay?" shrieked Jeanie.

I hung up the phone and was really looking forward to meeting Cheryl and Jeanie the next day.

When I walked into Robbies the next evening, Jeanie was yelling, "Diane, Diane, over here!"

Only instead of just Cheryl and Jeanie, it was Laurie, Beth, Pam, Cheryl, and Jeanie. I hung my coat on the hat tree by the door and self-consciously walked toward the table. I regretted my outfit immediately. I had worn a classic monochrome teacher look. My black Brighton flats, black tights, knee-length black wool skirt, and cream-colored turtleneck sweater screamed *boring*!

Cheryl had on a pair of stiletto-heeled brown boots with a short, green, belted sweater dress. Her long, brown, curly hair was pulled to the side in a loose ponytail. She popped up from her seat and gave me a hug, "Hey, Diane," she said, and then whispered, "this was Jeanie's idea."

Jeanie stood, put her arm around me, and introduced me to the girls around the table. She had on a similar outfit as mine, but she wore hers completely different. She had on black ballet flats, a very short, tight, black miniskirt, black tights, and a snug-fitting black turtleneck with a silver belt that was belted over the sweater around her narrow hips. Her large silver hooped earrings were accentuated by her frosted, gray, loose updo. She then dropped her arm, waved it around the table at the other girls, and said, "Welcome to the First Wives Club!"

Inspired by the movie, they had flippantly created their own First Wives Club during their recent twenty-five-year class reunion. They were commiserating about cheating husbands and divorce settlements, when Pam had commented she wished she'd had that conversation *before* her divorce. They had all agreed they could have benefited from each other's advice *before* their divorces. After that, they regularly met and discussed different issues specific to divorced women.

Beth was the first to introduce herself. She was plump with thick blonde hair cut in a layered bob and crystal-blue eyes. She wore little makeup, if any. She had a quiet, confident beauty about her and was very down to earth.

She offered her hand and said, "Hi, Diane, I'm Beth." She was a stockbroker and had recently been made a partner in a successful brokerage firm.

Pam was a tall, full-busted woman with no butt. She had an edgy short haircut and was showing lots of cleavage in a low-cut sweater. She offered her hand next, "I'm Pam. I've heard a lot of nice things about you." She was an accountant for a firm in Springfield.

Laurie was sitting back, watching the introductions unfold, when she smiled sweetly and said, "I'm Laurie. I own the coffee shop next door."

The waitress approached, and I gave her my drink order.

Pam said, "I think we have mutual friends or maybe enemies. My ex-husband is a high school teacher and coach. Your brother's ex-wife, Millie, teaches with him. We have two boys, and she sometimes babysits them when George has taken them to school."

"I can see her doing that; she loves kids. How old are your kids?"

"My boys are five and two. I divorced before the youngest was born."

Smiling, Cheryl said, "Tell her your story, Pam. I need a good laugh and never get tired of hearing you tell it."

"Well, one day I came home early, because my husband was on a school break, and my mom had our older son for the day. I was going to surprise him with the news I was pregnant. Only, I was the one who was surprised, when I walked into the kitchen and saw a woman's purse on the kitchen counter. I called out to my husband while I was walking back to our bedroom. I found him and some woman in our bed, hiding under the covers. He was pleading for me to go back into the kitchen, while the woman kept hidden under the covers. I lost it. I screamed at them to get out of my bed, but when they wouldn't budge, I walked back into the kitchen and rifled through her purse to find her driver's license. She was my dentist! I was so mad. I took her license, left the house, and tossed it into the lake as I crossed the bridge into town to clean out our bank accounts. Later I found out it hadn't been his first affair. We get along now, for the benefit of the boys."

Everyone laughed at the animated way she told the story.

"At least yours kept his job!" Beth said sarcastically. "My husband and I had gone to Duke University together and were both business majors. After college, I accepted a position in a small brokerage firm in North Carolina, while *my* husband proceeded to begin and end his career by bilking the corporation he worked for out of close to a million dollars. Thankfully, my firm didn't hold *his* actions against me and were actually instrumental, along with my parents, in helping me extricate myself from him and the lawsuits that followed. In the end, he was able to avoid jail time, because the secretary, *his girlfriend*, signed all the evidence. I consider myself lucky to be rid of him!"

"I miss the sex," said Laurie. "I walked away with a hefty settlement and full custody of my kids, but *I really* miss the sex. We had a great sex life, and he was the love of my life."

I could tell Laurie still had serious issues over her divorce. She didn't talk much about the details of the breakup, as much as she talked about sex, sex, and more sex.

I enjoyed getting to know each of the women and hearing their stories. I was thinking about their advice on the way home. The scariest piece, which resonated with me, was that I should divorce Don as soon as possible, while he was still in love with his *soul mate*. They felt a favorable settlement was imperative on catching him while he was still desperate to be with *her*.

As I pulled in the snow-covered drive, the dogs came bouncing toward me. They loved the snow and seemed happier with each other when it was cold, because they would lay wrapped around each other at night for warmth. I put the dogs up, set the alarm, and turned a comfy chair toward the snow-covered trees that were silhouetted by the moonlight. The deer were easy to spot against the white snow at the edge of the pond. As I sat there, lost in thought from the evening's conversations, I enjoyed nature's late-night show as different animals slipped out from the woods and came to the pond.

*   *   *

The following Saturday morning, Cheryl called.

I answered, "Hey, Cheryl."

"Hi. How ya doin'?" asked Cheryl.

"Fine. I slept late and am now enjoying a cup of coffee," I answered.

"I've been meaning to call you since the other night; I hope you didn't feel ambushed. I know that group can be overbearing, especially Jeanie; she has good intentions but does cross the line when it comes to personal boundaries," Cheryl said apologetically.

"Not at all!" I exclaimed. "I really enjoyed meeting everyone, and I'm looking forward to getting together again."

"Oh, well, good then, because Beth is hosting a happy hour at her house tonight, and she asked if I would call you to see if you could come."

"I'd love to. What should I bring?" I asked, wondering what I could put together on short notice.

"Everyone usually brings a bottle of what they want to drink and an appetizer to share," answered Cheryl. "I think Jeanie is bringing stuff from the med spa to do skin peels on everyone; it'll be fun."

"Does that hurt?" I asked curiously.

"No, not really, but I wouldn't wear anything that you don't want ruined, and I'd bring a headband to pull your hair back," she instructed.

"Okay. What time and where?" I asked, feeling adventurous.

"You live out in the country north of town don't you?" she asked.

I answered, "Yeah."

"Well, I'm on the north side too. Why don't we meet in the parking lot at Kroger? The parking will be tight at Beth's, and we can just ride together, if that's okay with you," Cheryl suggested.

"That would be great, thanks!" I replied with a bubbling excitement. "What time do you want to meet?"

"How 'bout six?" asked Cheryl.

"Perfect. I'll see you then," I said as I hung up.

As we pulled onto Beth's street, it was hard to find parking. Her house was built in the 1940s, when parking wasn't given much consideration. I loved her house immediately. It was a small, white Cape Cod with black shutters. The neatly shoveled brick path led from the drive to her red front door. As we stepped inside to a stone entryway, I felt . . . happy. The house exuded charm. When we walked down the hall to the kitchen in the back of the house, I could see the duck pond at Fairview Park through her cozy breakfast nook. The kitchen was a small galley-style kitchen with the original cherry cabinets and brass knobs. I noticed she had dog treats on her counter and looked around for a dog. We continued through an archway that opened to the dining room.

It had built-in corner cabinets and a gorgeous crystal chandelier. After adding our appetizers with the others on the table, we circled back to the front of the house through the pillared archway that led from the dining room to the large living room, which we had passed in the entryway. Beth was starting a fire in a stone fireplace that had an intricately carved mantel. "Beth, I love your house!" I gushed. "How long have you lived here?"

"Thanks. I love it too, although it does have stories," she said, enticing my imagination.

Others were coming in, and Beth went to take coats that wouldn't fit in the closet. I was fascinated to learn about the house's stories.

When Jeanie arrived, she instructed four at a time to sit in the breakfast nook as we cleansed our faces, and she gave instructions for the skin peels. I laughed and drank and left that night with smooth skin.

On the way home, I thought, *I laughed and had more fun tonight than I have in the last ten years.* I was still energized from the evening's events and wanted to share my news with someone, so I called Ellen, on my way home, to tell her about the party. After I told her about the party, she gave me the latest updates regarding their move to the Gulf Coast.

When I pulled up to the house, I noticed someone had plowed the drive. *Did Don plow the drive?*

Later that night, as I was seated in my comfy chair watching nature's show, I reflected on Beth's house. I could see myself living in her house. I loved that area of town. The houses in the historic district had always intrigued me from years ago when I sold real estate. Those were the houses I loved to tour. I began the mental exercise of buying a home in the historic district and let the impending sale of my dream home creep toward a reality. I knew I would have been a slave to the house after the divorce. I acknowledged for the first time that I was excited to look for another house. Not that I wouldn't miss my home; I would, but it wasn't the same living there by myself. The home needed a family to enjoy its full potential.

CHAPTER 8

Mick called a week or so after he returned from Colorado. I told him about my new club. He wasn't very talkative.

"What's the matter, Mick? You don't seem to have much to say tonight."

"It's just that I'm sitting here wondering if my soon-to-be ex is sitting around in some bar discussing how she can screw *me* over."

"I'm sorry, I shouldn't have told you all that."

"No, I'm happy you are making new friends. I'm just feeling like . . . I want to leave this town and start over. After being gone in Colorado and skiing those snow-covered mountains . . . and just being . . . anonymous . . . it felt so liberating. I came back here and ran into the little bozo my wife is shacking up with today. I've really been thinking about moving out to the East Coast. My folks still live there."

"Really? You would just leave your job? Can you transfer or something?" I asked, surprised.

"No, I'm sick of hospital work. I feel like a sellout most of the time. Hospitals and health care are all about a profit. When I started this job, it was about helping people," he said, sounding dejected.

"What would you do?" I asked, curious.

"I've been thinking, since 9/11, about working for the government, maybe doing something with my aviation background. I have a buddy from college who was encouraging me to move back to the DC area and work for the FBI."

"How would that affect your family here?"

"Well, let's see, I wouldn't have to see 'she who must not be named' or the little bozo she's with," he said, dripping with disgusted sarcasm.

I laughed at his *Harry Potter* reference. Initially, he had mocked me for reading *Harry Potter*, but he soon succumbed to the same addiction when he realized what a wonderful mental break that *Harry Potter* provided.

"My daughter has had the same boyfriend for the last six years, and they are both graduating from Purdue, in Indiana, with engineering degrees. John Deere, Intel, and 3M are recruiting her as we speak. So I'm not worried about her. My son is a CRNA, certified registered nurse anesthetist, in Colorado. He spends every spare minute on the slopes at Winter Park. And my brother and parents live in the DC area; so, if I move back, I'll have family, and my kids love visiting that area. Okay, now *you're* not very talkative," Mick prodded.

"Well, I'm impressed that you have a plan for your next chapter; no offense, you're over fifty and planning to start all over. It encourages me. I hadn't thought of the endless possibilities I could do to change *my* life."

Mick chuckled and said, "I haven't done it yet."

I wanted to do something nice for Mick, to pull him out of his slump, when I asked, "Would you like to come over for dinner sometime this week?"

"Sure. How 'bout now? I'm starving!" he asked hopefully.

"Well, if you came now, you would have your choice of a peanut butter and jelly sandwich or an egg sandwich, but, if you waited a couple of days, you could have a rib eye, baked potato, maybe a dessert, and a nice bottle of wine."

"I really like peanut butter and jelly," Mick teased.

"Yes, but then I'd have to jump in the shower, shave my legs, put on makeup, and pretend I look like that all the time," I said, and laughed.

"I could help you with that shower," Mick said playfully.

I laughed and said, "I think you are wanting more than a peanut butter and jelly sandwich now."

"Hey, I'm just trying to be helpful," he teased.

"How 'bout we plan for dinner on Thursday?" I said, rerouting the conversation as my stomach fluttered.

"That's a long time to wait, and I really have a craving for peanut butter and jelly," he said, insinuating he was craving more than that.

"I'm only offering dinner," I clarified, feeling unsure of what I was starting.

Mick laughed and said, "I'll bring the wine and see you at six."

Two days later, I was on the phone with Jeanie when Mick rang the doorbell. "Is that your doorbell?" Jeanie asked, surprised.

"It is, Jeanie. I'm going to have to let you go; maybe we can meet for a drink tomorrow," I said evasively.

"Who's at your door?" she asked curiously.

"Don's here to go over some paperwork," I lied.

"Why is he ringing your doorbell?" she pursued.

"Jeanie, he's going to be irritated if he's kept waiting," I pleaded, hoping she'd sympathize with my situation.

"Who cares; let him wait!" she spewed, disgusted.

"Jeanie, I'll call you tomorrow, bye," I said as I hung up on her.

I answered the door and said, "I'm sorry to keep you waiting. Jeanie was on the phone, and I had to lie to end the call."

"Oh, the tangled webs we weave, when first we practice to deceive," Mick teased, wagging his finger at me.

"Shut up," I said, and smiled.

Mick uncorked the bottle of wine he brought and asked, "Where are your wine glasses?"

"They're hanging under that cabinet," I said, pointing to the open butler's pantry. "I'll be right back. I'm going to put the dogs up before I throw these steaks on the grill."

"How about I put the steaks on the grill while you put up the dogs?"

"Okay, thanks." I missed the comfortable dance of preparing a meal with someone. After I put the dogs in the garage, I picked up a glass of wine and walked over to the chocolate dessert I had made from scratch. It had turned out perfect, and I presented it on my antique crystal cake stand. I was extremely proud of myself. I wiggled my eyebrows and tried to dazzle him with my chocolate dessert, when I said, "Check this out for dessert."

"*I am*," Mick said salaciously, wiggling his eyebrows back at me.

"You're bad," I said, and smiled.

"I promise, I'll be good," Mick teased in a low, sexy voice.

"You'd better turn those steaks; I like mine rare," I said, and laughed.

We enjoyed a leisurely dinner over a good bottle of wine and conversation. Mick was helping clear the dishes when he said suggestively, "I'm ready for more dessert." His low, quiet voice alluded to considerably more than dessert.

I could tell by the expression on his face he wasn't talking about my chocolate dessert anymore.

I was rinsing the dishes in the sink when Mick stepped behind me, leaned down circling his arms around my waist, and whispered in my ear, "Would you like more dessert?"

The vibration of his whisper and soft touch of his lips on my ear sent shockwaves down through my body. I could feel his arousal pressed in my back. My mind and libido were at odds with each other. Deeply suppressed sexual feelings were jolted awake.

"I don't think you know what dessert means," I answered, feeling insecure.

"You could explain it to me; I take directions well," Mick said, kissing my neck.

I can't do this! I'm not ready. But then again, I don't remember these feelings with Don. I wonder if it'll be different. I can't breathe; I need more space.

"How about we go upstairs and watch a movie," I said, thinking that would divert the conversation.

"I'd rather go into your bedroom," he continued calmly.

I froze. I still felt guilty for having him over; I didn't need to heap more guilt on myself by going to bed with him. *What if Don would find out and use it against me in the divorce? What if he has an STD? What if this is all he is after?*

"Chocolate cake was the only thing on the dessert menu, big boy," I said, pushing him back and trying to joke my way out of the situation.

"Menus change all the time," Mick said as he nuzzled my neck with soft kisses. "We could share a delicious dessert. You'll love it. I promise."

My libido was winning. When was the last time a man made me feel like a sexy woman instead of a cook and a mom?

The phone started ringing, and I stepped away from Mick, feeling like a teenager in her parents' kitchen.

Mick released a small groan.

"Why don't you see what's on TV," I said as I grabbed the phone.

"If we do, you can't talk during commercials," Mick said, mocking me.

We ended up watching the animals around the pond and talking over another piece of cake. An hour later, Mick said he needed to leave, and I walked him to the door. We embraced in a long kiss, and then he kissed the top of my head, smiled, and said, "Maybe, I'll bring *dessert* next time."

I gave a nervous laugh and said, "Call me later."

He looked back on the way to his car and said, "Oh, I will."

CHAPTER 9

The next week, we flew up to Chicago in his plane to see a Bulls basketball game. Even though I wasn't a sports fan, I enjoyed the sense of adventure. *Funny, I hated going to games with Don.*

Mick's divorce became a second job for him. *Her* lawyer had requested the last ten years of receipts for his airplane and taxes. He frequently had to speak with his lawyer because "she who must not be named" evidently wasn't cooperating.

My divorce was in the final stages, and I was busy with school and my own life. For years, our school had been negotiating consolidation with the small school district adjacent to us. The school boundaries, mascots, district name, grade sizes, and minute issues were so contentious that I didn't think consolidation would be a possibility. However, at the February board meeting, they had actually finalized negotiations for consolidation. My fifth-grade classroom would be moving ten miles down the road to Davidsonville Elementary, as my current school, Mayo Elementary, would only house kindergarten through fourth grade. Several of the current fourth-grade parents were upset because they felt their children were too young to be bused that far next year. They were protesting fifth grade's move to another town. I was taking a wait-and-see attitude. The thought of moving classrooms, Anna moving from the dorm to an apartment, Ellen moving to the Gulf Coast, me moving when I sell the house, and

Mick possibly moving to DC was more than I could think about just then.

Valentine's Day was in two days. The classrooms at school were decorated with pink and red hearts. Mick had invited me to go out of town for dinner, and my girlfriends had wanted me to join them in a Valentine Spa Night that Jeanie was sponsoring at the Med Spa where she worked. Both were good offers. I was a little anxious about Mick's offer and "dessert." My divorce would be final in a matter of weeks, but the idea of dessert still seemed a little ominous.

As I was taking my makeup off and getting ready for bed, I looked around my beautiful bathroom and thought, *I'm really going to miss this.* I was looking at the tub and fantasizing about soaking in the tub with Mick. Rose petals were floating in bubbles, and candles were lit around the tub. *Why couldn't I have that fantasy? I'm a grown woman, and I don't ever remember sitting in that tub with Don. I may never have the chance again for a romantic soak in this tub. What a waste!*

I started to plan a Valentine's Day that *I* wanted.

I called Mick to let him know I had a change of heart about going out of town on a school night. I could tell he was relieved. The only reason we were going out of town was to avoid people, and adding a two-hour drive to a dinner didn't appeal to either of us. I told him that I would cook, and he said he'd bring the wine.

The next day, Mick rang the bell at 7:00 p.m. and presented me with a dozen red and white roses. *Good start.* He smelled wonderful and looked very GQ in a gray suit and blue dress shirt that had little sailboat cuff links.

"You look cute," Mick said as he bent down to give me a quick peck. I had on a bright, coral-colored, short, polo shirt-dress, with nothing underneath.

"I'm definitely underdressed compared to you," I said curiously, hoping he remembered we weren't going out.

"I had a presentation before the board today and didn't have an opportunity to change," he explained.

"Well, you look very nice, Mr. Ashmore," I teased in a formal tone.

"Well, thank you, Ms. Miller," he said, teasing me in a Rhett Butler fashion.

"This is for you," he said as he handed me the flowers, a bottle of wine, and a box of chocolates.

"Thank you," I said as I took the bottle into the kitchen and put the flowers in a vase.

I opened the bottle and grabbed two glasses. I had already had two vodka tonics to muster the courage for the night. I had Sade playing in the background and was feeling comically confident.

"I thought we'd start by just relaxing with a couple of drinks," I said.

I nearly burst out laughing, but I contained it to a smile. Mick looked at me curiously and loosened his tie.

"That sounds great to me; this has been a long day," he said, visibly relaxing.

"Well, let's start with my favorite way to relieve stress," I said, indicating for him to follow me.

I started giggling at the look on his face as we headed toward my bedroom. When we walked into my bathroom, he saw all the lit candles. The bath was bubbling with rose petals and lavender-scented bubbles. A small crystal bowl of chocolates, a plate of assorted cheese and crackers, and a blue cooler were tucked to the side.

His look of total shock fueled my next move. In one swift motion, I set down my glass of wine, pulled the hem of my dress over my head, stepped into the bath and sat in bubbles up to my neck, picking up my glass again.

Mick's eyebrows shot up, his eyes widened the size of quarters, and his mouth dropped open. He was just standing there with his glass of wine looking at me.

"Would you like to relax with me while we enjoy our wine?" I said casually, as if I'd asked to take his coat.

"Yes, I would," he replied matter-of-factly as he removed his clothes. He wasn't shy, and it is true what they say about big hands and feet. As he sat down, the overflow started draining in the tub.

Mick sat at one end of the tub, covered in bubbles, with his wine and a big grin. I sat opposite him, at the other end of the tub, wearing a satisfied smirk as I raised my glass in a toast.

"Here's to being us!"

We toasted and talked, as if we were sitting at the kitchen table. We had finished the bottle of wine, and Mick was sweating from the heated tub.

"As much as I hate to say this, I need to get out; I'm overheated," he said apologetically.

I reached around for my blue cooler and pulled out the container of still-frozen Breyers chocolate ice cream with two spoons.

"I have a cure for that," I said as I handed him a spoon and turned off the jets, so the bath would cool down. "Dessert first," I said, wiggling my eyebrows.

Mick burst out laughing. He took the spoon, and we ate ice cream in the tub.

Mick asked, smiling, "Is this dinner?"

"No, I made you something you told me a while back that you really liked," I said, trying to sound serious but fighting a smile.

After a while, Mick looped his leg over the side of the tub and grabbed one of the towels that I'd laid on the vanity.

He handed me the towel and, in what sounded like a dare, said, "My turn to see yours; you've already seen mine."

I laughed and said, "You saw mine; I undressed first."

"Not fair; it lasted less than five seconds, and I blinked and missed it!" he said, sounding like a little boy who'd dropped the ice cream from his cone.

I burst out laughing because what he said was the truth.

I took the towel and wrapped it around me as I stood up and then stepped from the tub, over to the vanity.

"You are not playing fair," he teased, feeling cheated at another brief glimpse.

When Mick stood up and grabbed a towel, it was obvious what his plans were next. He reached his arms around me and looked at our reflection in the mirror.

"We could send this picture out as a Christmas card, don't you think?" Mick asked, teasing.

"Your towel is making it X-rated," I said, referring to his bulge.

He grabbed his towel and said, "I'll just take it off then."

Before I could think, he had swooped me up and was lying on top of me in bed, when he said, "There, is that better?"

For the next hour, I let all my inhibitions go. Neither one of us had been with anyone for so long that each touch was like the first time. My senses were besieged by feelings and sensations I don't think I'd ever felt before. It was overwhelming. Afterward, I thought, *A woman should only depend on a man for intimacy.*

After a long, silent embrace, Mick asked, "What are we having for dinner?"

I laughed and said, "You'll see; you told me that you really liked it."

I threw my shirt-dress back on, over my underwear, and went into the kitchen while Mick dressed. He came out in dress slacks and a shirt.

"So where is this dinner?" he asked, starting to doubt its existence.

I pulled the rounded silver cover off the plate and said, "Peanut butter and jelly sandwiches."

He laughed, picked up a peanut butter and jelly sandwich, and said, "This is actually the best Valentine's dinner I have ever had."

I couldn't have agreed more as I opened the box of chocolates he'd brought and pinched the bottoms to find my favorites.

Chapter 10

February 17, almost six months to the day of finding out Don was having an affair, I was sitting on a wooden chair, with my hand raised, swearing that I would tell the truth before a judge that, within minutes, would end my marriage. To make it easier on each of us, Don agreed not to go to court. The details were all worked out, and since I had filed, I was the only person that needed to show up in court to make it final. The dialogue in my head did not match the proceedings around me.

The first question from the judge was "Mrs. Miller, are you pregnant at this time?"

I answered "No." But I was thinking, *What the hell?*

The judge was a middle-aged black woman who could have been reading a grocery list, as easily as she was ticking off the remnants of my marriage. It was a surreal moment. I didn't tell anyone, except Anna and Mick, my court date was that day. Up until that moment, I was feeling confident and strong. Don had been very generous with me, and my life was moving forward.

When the judge rapped her gavel and said, "Let the record show Don and Diane Miller are now legally divorced," I questioned whether my knees would be able to carry me out of the courtroom. I was visibly shaking when the officer extended his hand toward me, indicating it was time to step down. I left the courthouse, went home, changed into walking shoes, and stepped onto the treadmill downstairs for a long walk with Harry

Potter. The fantasy world of Hogwarts allowed me the mental break I needed from all the stress of the divorce.

*   *   *

Anna called and asked hesitantly, "So is it official?"

"Yeah," I said with a sigh.

"How was it?" she asked anxiously.

"It was just a matter of going in before a judge and signing a paper," I answered resolutely.

"That doesn't sound too bad," she answered, sounding hopeful.

"No, it was fine. The marriage ended when he left; this was just paperwork," I said, acting as if it was no big deal.

We talked awhile and caught up on the latest about Ellen's move and SIU news. She had decided dorm living wasn't for her. She had made plans with Becky, Carrie, and Holly, a girl she'd met in the dorm, to find an apartment in the fall.

*   *   *

Mick stopped over later that night with Krekel's hamburgers, fries, and chocolate milk shakes.

"Comfort food," Mick said, handing me the bag.

"Thank you." That was the first thing I had had to eat all day. I really wasn't hungry, until I smelled the fries and eyed the chocolate shake. We carried the bags upstairs to eat in front of the TV.

"How did it go today?" he asked, curious.

"Kind of like . . . getting your wisdom teeth pulled. You go in, sit down, it hurts like hell, but you're kind of numb through it all, and you walk away feeling an emptiness," I answered, feeling a wave of exhaustion.

"That gives me something to look forward to," he said facetiously.

We sat on the couch together, munching on fries and watching mindless TV most of the evening. That night he didn't leave until morning.

*   *   *

Anna came home, in April, for spring break. I had come to the decision I would put the house on the market after she returned to SIU from spring break; after all, spring was the best time to sell a house.

Two days after Anna had left for SIU, the sign went into the front lawn. The real estate agent, Glenda, cautioned me that the market was very slow and that most people weren't buying in my price range. She had hoped we would find an out-of-town buyer and wanted to schedule an open house the following Sunday. There wasn't much preparation I needed to do. The house was clean, and with just me at home, it would stay that way. The agent had just left, and I was staring out at the sign in the front yard with mixed emotions. I was exhilarated at the thought of my independence and a fresh start in a new house but was still a little scared to let go of the familiar. I was thinking about all the possibilities, when the phone interrupted my thoughts.

"Hi, Diane, it's Glenda. I just talked to an agent in my office, and he was wondering if he could show your house. He was showing his clients houses out in that area, when they saw me put the sign in the yard."

"Sure, when does he want to show it?" I asked casually.

"Actually, they want to come now, if that's okay," Glenda said timidly.

"That's fine, Glenda, the house is ready to show," I replied.

"Do you think you could leave while they show it?" she asked cautiously.

I sold real estate; I knew houses showed better when the owners were gone. I just wasn't sure what to do about the dogs.

"What do you think I should do about the dogs?" I asked. She knew, firsthand, that the dogs would jump on the prospective buyers and their cars.

"Is there any way you can take them with you?" Glenda pleaded.

"I don't think so, Glenda; we usually put them in the back of a truck. I'd be afraid they'd trash my car," I said apologetically. "What about if I just close them in the garage, and we warn the agent not to let them out. They can peek in the garage with them in there. I'm sure they are just looking to be looking, since they are out this way anyway. If they're really interested, I'll put the dogs up next time they come back."

"Okay, I'll call him back and tell him," she assured me.

I left the house and headed into town, to Target. On the way, I called Cheryl to see if she wanted to meet me for a drink, but her machine answered instead. After Cheryl, I tried Jeanie, but she didn't answer either. I was walking around Target when my phone rang.

"Hey, what's going on?" I answered, assuming it was either Cheryl or Jeanie.

"Hi, Diane, this is Glenda," she clarified excitedly. "I just finished talking to the other agent, and he is writing a contract on your house! He wants to know if all the pillows, ottomans, and bed skirts in the bedrooms, which match the window treatments, stay with the house."

"What?" I asked, shocked. "I don't know," I stuttered. I was completely taken off guard. "How much are they offering?"

"I don't know the offer yet; he just asked about the custom window treatments and all the coordinating accessories. They loved the house. They want to know if you will be selling any of the furniture," replied Glenda encouragingly.

"Well, let's just say it's negotiable, at this point, until we see the offer," I said with as much conviction as I could find. I needed to sit down; I was having trouble concentrating with the commotion in the background.

"Okay. Where are you?" inquired Glenda.

"I'm at Target," I responded. "I think I need to call Don."

"Okay," responded Glenda anxiously, "I'll plan on, tentatively, meeting you back at your house in an hour and a half, unless you hear back from me."

I called Don's cell, but he seemed reluctant to meet me at the house.

"You really don't need me there, Diane, since the equity in the house is yours; you can decide whether to take the offer," he said, indicating he wasn't going to participate.

"But what if they have questions that I can't answer about the house?" I asked, feeling a panicked sense of abandonment.

"*You* sold real estate; you're more familiar than I am with real estate contracts," he reasoned.

We were divorced; I couldn't expect him to come running just because I called. It seemed to be a major decision to be making by myself. I couldn't shake the feeling that I needed someone with me for the negotiation. *I'm a big girl. I can do this.*

Don filled in the silent pause with a reminder, "Diane, you used to say, 'The first offer is the best offer,' so, if it's close to what we're asking, take it. The sooner the house sells, the closer we will be to ending all this drama."

I knew he was right, but his words cut through me like a knife, and I didn't have time for hurt feelings.

An hour later, Glenda and I were sitting on one side of my kitchen table, and the other real estate agent, John Camden, was sitting opposite us presenting the contract.

"My buyers are moving here from the St. Louis area. The husband is being transferred here by ADM. They have two young boys; one is in third and the other in fifth grade. I told him that you taught fifth grade. But you don't teach in this school district, do you?"

"No, I don't," I said, but was thinking, *Will you get to the price!*

"They have always wanted a piece of property like this. They will be putting 50 percent down, so financing isn't going to be a problem with them. This is a very good contract."

Finally, he put the contract on the table between us.

"As you can see, it is a full-priced contract with a ninety-day closing of July 15. They have included all the window treatments and appliances. We wrote this separate addendum that includes all the custom bedding, accessories, and living room pillows, but I told them those were all negotiable. They wanted me to ask you for the person's number who made all the accessories that coordinate with the window treatments, in case you were going to take them with you. They loved the entire house. As a matter of fact, they are interested in buying all the furniture in the great room and the kitchen's breakfast nook. They just thought the whole back of this house was so spectacular, with the way all the windows overlook the pond, that they don't want to change one thing."

There really wasn't anything to negotiate. I signed the contract but told him that I wouldn't sign the addendum until I found another house, to see if I might still be able to use my custom bedding and accessories. I gave him the number of Blanche, the interior designer I had used, so that they could duplicate them if they chose later. I shook hands with Mr. Camden and walked him to the door. Glenda was so excited; she screeched and gave me a whooping hug. I could see the dollar signs dancing in her eyes; that was probably the easiest commission she had ever earned. I couldn't share her excitement. I felt the weight of all the packing and moving, with the added pressure of finding another house, coming at me like a freight train.

After Glenda left, I called Don to tell him the news, but he let my call go to voice mail. I hesitated whether to leave a message and thought with a sigh, *What does it really matter?*

"Don, this is Diane. I signed a contract on the house tonight, with a closing date of July 15. We'll need to decide what to do with all the stuff in this house," I said in a monotone.

I went into my closet, sat on the floor, and had a good cry. The phone rang, but I didn't care. I had a full-blown pity party for myself. I felt like everything was slipping from me. The divorce was final, Anna had just left, my classroom was moved to a new school, my house was being sold, Ellen had found a house and was moving to the coast, and Mick was seriously contemplating leaving too. After a while, I was cried out and decided to end the party.

Someone was still calling. I left my closet and answered the phone.

"Hello," I said, trying to sound like I hadn't been crying.

"Where have you been?" asked Ellen, irritated.

I heaved a heavy sigh, to steady my voice and tell her the house sold, but when I started to tell her, my voice broke into choked sobs.

"What's the matter? Are you all right? What are you saying?" Ellen asked frantically.

"I'm fine. I'm upset because the house sold tonight," I said, trying to manage my emotions.

"Did that bastard make you take a low price?" Ellen scathed.

"No, he didn't even show up to hear the offer or even take my call later, to let him know how it went," I said, feeling hurt and offended, all over again.

Ellen was stunned into a moment of silence, until she said, "What did it sell for?"

"Full price, with a closing on July 15; it couldn't be better," I said grudgingly, knowing I should be grateful.

"You should have asked more!" Ellen exclaimed.

I laughed. "You were the one who said I listed it too high in the first place!" I exclaimed incredulously.

"Well, it's all meant to be," Ellen said, trying to sound conciliatory.

"I know," I said, starting to cry again, "it just feels as if I'm losing everything, though."

"You're not losing anything; it's just changing, and the only thing certain in life is change. You've gotta believe that everything works out for the best," Ellen said, trying to assuage the situation.

"Okay, enough with the clichés; I'm not suicidal! I'm just trying to process all this. Four hours ago, I thought I'd be here for possibly another year. Reality is just coming at me a little fast tonight."

"Well, I'm glad you're not suicidal, because I probably have really bad timing then. Do you want to hear 'the latest and greatest' about Don and Carol?"

"Might as well!"

"They got married this afternoon, at the justice of the peace, and are flying off to some place in the Caribbean for their honeymoon," Ellen spat out quickly, in one breath.

I started laughing at the absurdity of it all.

"Well, that explains why he wouldn't take my call or meet me for the contract," I said, feeling a degree of relief.

"Are you okay?" Ellen asked hesitantly.

"Yes. I was just wondering if Anna knew," I said, disheartened.

"Are you going to call her?" Ellen asked curiously.

"I don't know what I'm going to do. I may just go back to my pity party, for a while, and take a long, hot bath," I said, resigning to do just that.

I sank into the lavender-scented bubbles, equipped with all my spa masks and soaps, and thought about the last time I was in there, on Valentine's Day.

CHAPTER 11

A few days later, when I had my emotions under control, I called Anna.

"Hi, honey, what are you doing?" I chirped cheerfully, genuinely happy to hear her voice.

"Becky is over, and she's helping me pick out an outfit. I'm going out with somebody new tonight," she said expectantly.

"Where did you meet him?" I asked, stalling for time from the news I had to deliver.

"I met him at the Driver's License Bureau," she said, hedging her words.

"Why were you at the Driver's License Bureau?" I asked, knowing there was much more to the story, if I cared to pursue.

"I had to give Becky a ride; she lost her driver's license and had to apply for a new one," Anna lied.

I knew she was lying, but she would tell me the truth about what Becky had done later, when she was alone.

I hesitated and said, "So . . . I have some news, when you have a chance to talk."

"I think I know, Mom," Anna answered soberly.

"About your dad?" I asked, feeling a bit of betrayal that she knew.

"They're married, aren't they?" she asked, but I sensed she didn't want to hear the certainty.

"Yes. Ellen called and said they were married at the justice of the peace and then honeymooning in the Caribbean," I said as matter-of-factly as possible. "Did you know?" I asked, trying to keep the hurt from my voice.

Damn it, why did I have to ask her that!

"He told me over spring break that they were going to be married shortly, but I didn't know the exact date," she said sympathetically. "I told him that I didn't want to hear anything about it," she said defiantly.

I conceded to myself that she was in an awkward position, and I continued delivering the rest of my news, hoping to alleviate the guilt I was causing her.

"The house sold, too. Full price to the first person who looked at it," I said, trying to sound positive.

"What? When do we have to move?" she asked, alarmed.

"Not until July 15. It'll be fine. You'll be home way before that, and we can look for another house," I said, faking optimism.

"What about Jack and Jill?" her voice rose anxiously.

I sighed and said, "I don't know. I was thinking I wanted to look for a house in the historic district, but Jack wouldn't function well in the city. Jill would, but I don't want to break them up. I'd love to find someone in the country that would take them both," I said, willing my voice to sound nonchalant, but my emotions were starting to betray me.

"You are *not* seriously thinking of getting rid of Jack and Jill," she said incredulously.

"I need to find a house first, and then I'll make that decision," I said, trying to placate her mood.

"This makes me so mad at Dad," she grumbled hatefully.

"It'll all work out for the best. You'll see. Consider this summer an adventure," I said encouragingly.

I could hear her relaying our conversation to Becky.

"Hey, Anna, I'll let you and Becky talk. Call me tomorrow; I want to hear the details of how your date goes tonight," I said, sensing my supportive-mother role crumbling at the imminent events.

"Okay. Love you, Mom."

"Love you too, honey."

I am not going to cry. I refuse to go to another pity party. I decided to do something for myself that day.

*   *   *

Forty-five minutes later, I was sitting in a vibrating chair, with my feet soaking in warm bubbles. I was relaxing with a gossip magazine in one of the two chairs that were set into a small, cozy alcove designed for pedicures. I had the good fortune of walking in on a Saturday, to an exclusive salon, and snagging a cancellation. I was enjoying reading about someone else's drama, when I heard a familiar voice. I looked up to see Caroline Wilkey. She was being ushered to the chair that was less than six inches from me, and we spent the next sixty minutes side by side. It might as well been sixty hours.

"Hi, Caroline," I said as sweetly as a southern woman masks contempt. Southern women have made an art out of delivering stinging barbs with a graceful smile and sweetness dripping from perfectly painted lips.

"Hi, Diane," she said, visibly scared. I could see her warring between an exit strategy and her sacred pedicure.

I was *also* warring with "Good Diane and Bad Diane." Bad Diane was saying, "*She's trapped now; let her have it. She has spread all kinds of gossip about you and Don; she's even had Carol and Don over for dinner. Tell her off!*"

Good Diane was saying, "*Take the high road. She was in an awkward position. Her husband has worked out with Don for years.*"

Bad Diane countered, "*Yes, and probably knew all about the affair this whole time, and she has been a total hypocrite to you, pretending to be your friend over the last year!*"

"So how have you been, Caroline?" I said sweetly, continuing to summon my inner southern woman.

"Fine. I've been so busy," stammered Caroline, trying to justify why she hadn't called me.

Her pedicurist, oblivious to the facts, piped up and said, "You all know each other?" My pedicurist must have known the background, or probably had listened to Caroline spreading all the gossip, because she hadn't said a word. She was concentrating on my toes as if she was performing a delicate surgery.

"Oh, I understand how busy you all are," I said, the double entendre making her more uncomfortable. My inner southern woman was standing in her high-heeled stilettos and push-up bra, smiling. *Bring it on, honey!*

I could tell she was trying to read my intentions before she responded, but I just smiled at her and pretended to be engrossed in my magazine.

Her peppy pedicurist seemed to feel the need to fill the silence and asked, "How do you all know each other?"

My inner southern woman jumped in before I could stop her. "Oh, we've known each other for years. I even stayed a week in a Colorado hospital with her, when she broke her foot and was in traction. I had stayed so she wouldn't be alone since our husbands needed to return to work. We were in each other's weddings; we've watched our kids grow up together. Do you remember that time when all three of your kids and you had the flu, and I came over and put your kids in that tub of ice? What a scene!"

Her pedicurist chirped, "It's so nice to see women like you all, who have stayed friends all these years and share so many memories. I hope that I get to do that some day."

Caroline hadn't said a word but clearly received the message.

My pedicurist had already massaged my calves and feet longer than the allotted time. She was soaking up every bit of the conversation to repeat later. I didn't care, if it meant a thoroughly meticulous pedicure. My inner southern woman relaxed and went to her happy place. Caroline, on the other hand, nervously commenced a series of tedious subjects trying to engage me in a conversation.

My inner southern woman refused to budge from her happy place and would only, occasionally, acknowledge Caroline with an obligatory nod and a smile.

Caroline's pedicure was finished before mine. I could see the distress it caused her.

"Well, it was good to see you, Diane," she said with a confused look.

"You take care," my inner southern woman said with a wide, energetic smile and still holding her gossip rag.

After she left, my pedicurist said, "I'm so sorry about that. Normally, we are very careful about who is seated next to each other back here. But, since it was a cancellation, I didn't make the connection until it was too late."

I could tell she was sincerely sorry; it wasn't her fault. I didn't want her feeling guilty.

"Don't think another thing about it; I'm not," I said, to calm the anxious look on her face. I gave her a very generous tip, hoping that at least when she retold the conversation in the salon that I would fare better than Caroline.

CHAPTER 12

On the drive home, I was feeling more confident and thinking about the move. Realizing my days were numbered in the house, I decided I wasn't going to grieve losing my house. I was going to celebrate my time there. I was going to plan a party before I had to pack everything. It was late April, and spring was budding all around the pond and in the woods. The flowerbeds under the trees that shaded the front of the house had hundreds of green sprouts from the tulip and daffodil bulbs. I planned to have a good-bye party for the house in May.

That Friday evening, I put the dogs in the garage with all-day chew bones. People would be arriving for the party any minute. I wasn't sure how many people were actually coming, as I had sent out an impromptu mass e-mail to friends and family, to join me for a last drink, letting them know the house had sold. It was a gorgeous spring evening. Flowers, bursting with color, surrounded the house and peppered the woods across the pond.

The scents wafting from the honeysuckle and lilac bushes, on the edge of the woods, were intoxicating from the back porch. The pond provided the perfect backdrop to the white Adirondack table and chairs on the dock. Various coolers of iced beer and water bottles were punctuated between the dock and the back porch.

Inside the house, my kitchen island was laden with appetizers. The open butler's pantry, which separated the dining room and kitchen, provided a bar that could be easily accessed from the front or back of the house. A generous assortment of liquor and a stocked wine rack filled a portion of the counter space, along with a coffeepot with cups, and a tray holding cream and sugar. I debated whether to use plastic cups or the stemware hanging from the rack under the upper cabinets of the butler's pantry. *Why not? It'll probably be the last party I have here!* I started placing the stemware next to the wine rack, when Mick walked in the back door.

"Hey, the back looks great. Do you need some help there?" asked Mick cheerfully.

"Okay! Can you pull the dog food out of the garbage cans, in the garage, and line them with plastic bags, then put the cans, inconspicuously, around the backyard?" I asked in teacher mode.

"I was hoping for one of those glasses and opening the wine," Mick laughed. "But I'll do refuse detail; it sounds like a better deal," Mick teased.

I smiled at him and said, "It is."

After arranging the stemware, I walked outside to check the placement of the garbage cans. "How did you place the cans?" I asked Mick.

"Inconspicuously," mocked Mick.

"So how do you feel about me meeting your friends and family today?" teased Mick playfully.

"Most of my friends know about you, and I'm sure Ellen has told my family all about you," I said, feeling less confident than I was letting on.

"And what do they know about me?"

"You're still married. We're friends that are commiserating together through a difficult time in our lives," I said, trying to decide if I was convincing him or myself.

"Okay. I just wanted to know what to say when all your single girlfriends start hitting on me," Mick said, and smiled sarcastically.

"You say you're still married," I smiled, even phonier, with equal sarcasm.

Before we could continue, my parents pulled into the drive. Mom was carrying a dish, and dad was walking behind her.

Dad said with a genuine smile, "The place looks great; I should have brought my fishing pole!"

Before I could make introductions, Mom grabbed Mick's cheek and pulled him down to her, where she gave him a kiss and said, "I've heard a lot of nice things about you, young man, even though my daughter hasn't said one word."

"Well, you can believe it, because it's all true," Mick teased back casually.

Mom laughed and started toward the kitchen. "I need to refrigerate this dessert. I made Robert Redford cake," she said, smiling.

Ellen told Mom!

I had told Ellen, a while back, how handsome I thought Mick was, and that he resembled Robert Redford. Years before I met Mick, a friend had given me a chocolate recipe, nicknamed "Robert Redford cake," in place of its name, "chocolate luscious layered cake." It was a private joke with Ellen that I had made that dessert the first time Mick came over for dinner.

Before I could think of a response, others had arrived, and I went back out to greet them and make introductions. The circle drive was filling, as friends and family were mingling, enjoying the dock area, and walking around the pond. Some had ventured onto the mulched trails in the woods; others were hanging out on the back porch, and many more were exploring the house. I didn't mind; that's what the party was about, saying my good-byes to the house and grounds with my family and friends.

The overall effect, from the color of all the flowers to the summer scents of the honeysuckle and lavender, was not wasted on my guests. I enjoyed seeing the amazed looks as everyone took in the backyard when they arrived. It was as if Mother Nature had decided to put on a grand finale for all of us that night.

"The First Wives Club" had arrived together. Beth was the first to comment, "Diane, this is like a beautiful nature preserve."

I knew she would have an appreciation for the property.

"Thank you. Would you like a tour?" I offered.

"I would love it!" she said excitedly. We went inside, passing my mom and Mary, who had been cheerfully giving tours most of the evening. When we reached the great room, Beth gasped, "Oh Diane, this view is magnificent! This woodwork and molding are usually only found in older homes."

I could sense that Beth felt my connection to the house by the way she looked around and ran her hands along the wood in the archways and on the railings.

She took my hand and said, "I'm so sorry you have to leave this house. I can see the care and attention you have poured into it. But you're going to find another one that needs your love just as much, and, if you'd like, I'll help you find it."

"Thank you, Beth," I said, encouraged by her comments.

As we finished the tour of the house, I looked around for Mick, worried I had neglected him, when I saw him sitting with Jeanie. Jeanie was flipping her hair, giggling, and had her hand on his thigh. Before I could move in that direction, Ellen and Mom had seen it too and were making a beeline in that direction. I laughed to myself. *We may not communicate much, but we do have each other's back.*

The girls from work were in the kitchen. Yolie was laughing with Deb about something, when I walked up.

"Hey, thanks for coming, guys," I said to the group in general.

"Your home is beautiful, Diane; I've never been here," said Deb. "We think you should host the end-of-school happy hour here with these leftovers."

"Nothing I'd like better," I said truthfully. School was out the following Tuesday, and Yolie began to make plans for the happy hour; wherever she was, there was a party. "Keep in mind, after today, the house will, hopefully, be partially packed in boxes," I said.

"Speaking of packing," Dena chimed in, "I saw a truckload of boxes outside the janitor's closet. Do you have to pack up your classroom by yourself?"

The conversation turned to school news and consolidation gossip. I stepped away, after a bit, to refresh a platter on the island, and headed back outside.

I looked out at the dock and saw my brothers talking to Mick. It looked as if they had found some fishing poles in the garage and were throwing a line off the dock. We had been throwing our Christmas trees in the pond, opposite from where they had their lines. If they wanted to catch fish, they needed to take the paddleboat across the pond to where the crappie were hiding under the trees.

My parents were visiting with Roger and Mary out by the garden. Roger didn't plant a garden that year but was still looking over the soil. He was probably saying his good-byes to the garden.

Toward the end of the evening, people began leaving, and, before long, the few that were left were helping bring in the garbage cans and coolers. In all, probably fifty-five people or so had come to the party. I was happy that I had the opportunity to enjoy one more party and that Mother Nature had provided such incredible decorations. I felt extremely satisfied with the evening's events. We had cleaned up outside, and I let the dogs out to run around for a while before I put them in again for the night.

When everyone but Mick had left, we sat at the kitchen table, eating a piece of Robert Redford cake, sharing different conversations that we'd had with others throughout the evening.

I said, "I was talking to my friend Karen, and she said that when she'd told her husband about Don, he said, 'That poor bastard, he should have gone out and bought a Harley. It would have been a lot cheaper.'" We laughed.

"Who is Karen? She looked familiar," asked Mick.

"She teaches high school at South River; your kids probably had her."

"Yeah, that's right, I remember her." Mick continued. "Your friend, Jeanie, was filling me in on my ex's supposed affairs. Your sister interrupted her from telling all the sordid details. I was glad, after hearing her, though, that I'd had myself tested after my ex left."

Yeah, it was easy for him; he was tested by one of his doctor friends at the hospital, confidentially.

*   *   *

I remember when I had my yearly appointment with my gyno and discreetly told the doctor that I had just rid myself of a cheating husband, and I wanted to be tested to make sure he didn't leave me any "parting gifts."

The doctor had walked out to the hall, and I heard him through the paper-thin door say to the nurse or technician, "This is from room four; it needs to be tested for STDs."

I cringed and wanted to crawl under my paper blanket.

*   *   *

"My older sister, Anne, was telling me about this drunk couple at the Mexican restaurant in town," I said. "She said the woman was loud and falling out of the booth, but she could only see the back of the man. They were trying to ignore them, but when the couple walked by to leave, it was Don and Carol. I guess Don was red-faced and wouldn't acknowledge my sister."

We continued sharing stories for a while. Later, before Mick left, he reminded me that he was taking the following week to visit his family in DC and explore career opportunities.

Chapter 13

I was so exhausted from packing the house that when I closed my eyes at night, all I could see were boxes. On the Friday following the last day of school, I thought the school building would be empty. I decided to go into my classroom and pack my personal belongings. I was busy packing when the enormity of starting all over again at a new school, on top of starting over in my personal life, overwhelmed me. I hadn't eaten, was tired, and could feel the wave of self-pity washing over me. I was trying not to cry. I took a deep breath to calm myself but let out a sob instead. I was looking for a tissue when Yolie walked into my room.

Yolie had taught at Mayo for longer than anyone else. She was probably close to sixty but acted seventeen. She was an attractive, older, black woman with big, expressive eyes. She had lost her husband a few years back to cancer. She had three grown children and eight grandchildren and was deeply devoted to her first-graders. Every year on Dr. Seuss's birthday she dressed up like the Cat in the Hat and read Dr. Seuss books to the students during their lunch. She was upbeat and energetic, with a boisterous personality. She had a heart of gold and an infectious laugh you could hear from down the hallway. She was also our school's representative for the teachers' union.

Yolie came in, put her arm around me, and asked sympathetically, "Girlfriend, what are you crying about?"

Blowing my nose, I said, "I'm sorry. I'm just feeling sorry for myself."

"You don't need to tell *me* you're sorry, I've seen the weight you've carried for the last year; you were bound to drop some of it."

"The thought of packing and starting all over again is just so exhausting," I said, feeling defeated.

"Well, why are *you* packing all this?" she asked, surprised.

"Because I need to sort out the junk I don't want, and I want boxes packed by centers."

"Honey, your contract ended on the last day of school. This isn't your problem. You wait here. I'm going to find the custodian; *he's* paid to work over the summer." Yolie came back with the custodian, Mr. Brown, in tow.

Yolie started giving orders to Mr. Brown. "She needs all this packed up. I'm going to help her label boxes, and you need to pack the boxes according to the labels on the outside. You need to start setting those flat boxes up and taping them now, so that we can put labels on them and place them in the labeled areas."

Yolie was in full teacher mode. To my amazement, he started doing everything she told him. We labeled a couple of boxes for my desk and a few other boxes for personal items that I wanted to be able to locate. She told him to label the rest, after they were packed, and to call me if there were any complications. She handed me my purse, and we walked down to her room.

"Thank you for doing that, Yolie. You're the only one he would have taken orders from like that; I think he's afraid of you."

"Oh, honey, can I give you some advice?"

"Yeah," I said. "Sure." I respected Yolie.

"People treat you how you let them treat you," she said. "Mr. Brown isn't any different than your ex-husband. You need to tell that ex to pack up that house and sell what needs to be sold. And while you are at it, *he* was the one who wanted those dogs. You've been stressing out over those dogs for too long. That should be *his* problem. You tell him that *he* needs to figure out what to do with those dogs. I'm sorry, honey, but taking charge of your life doesn't mean you have to do everything by yourself."

I gave Yolie a hug and said, "I'm going to miss you next year."

*   *   *

When I pulled in the drive, Jack and Jill were playing tug of war with a package that the UPS man had left on the front porch. *Damn it!* I *am* going to call Don and tell him that he is going to find a new home for these dogs. As I pulled in the garage, and saw the snowmobile, gator, four-wheeler, chest freezer, extra refrigerator, and all the other crap that needed to go, I thought, *And he is going to figure out a new home for all of this shit too!*

"Hi, Don. It's Diane." *Of course, I was leaving a message.* "I can't pack this house by myself. You need to clear the garage and the basement. I was thinking, if you rented a separate storage unit, we'd put any furniture Anna wants for her apartment in there, along with the things you want. I'm planning on you picking Anna up from school on May 31 with your truck and a U-Haul. Call me or just come out and start on it. Oh, and since you were the one who had to have the dogs, they are going with you when I move, so you should find a place for them if you don't want them."

By the time he brought Anna home a week later, Don had cleared out the basement and had made a concerted effort to clear the garage. He had done everything I had asked him to do as if it was his penance. I appreciated his efforts and enjoyed the truce. Even though I wasn't going to admit it, I knew that he had found someone he truly loved and that he wasn't intentionally trying to hurt me. I knew Don was a good man and would probably do anything I asked him to do. I didn't want conflict in my life anymore. I knew, deep down, I had forgiven him, but I wasn't ready to let him off the hook yet. I wanted to punish him a bit longer with his own guilt.

CHAPTER 14

One Saturday morning in June, I was mowing the front lawn, on the riding lawn mower, thinking about all the houses Glenda had showed me. We had seen close to forty houses in the last weeks. All the houses were starting to run together in my mind. I didn't feel as if we were on the same page to find what I was looking for in a home. She seemed to be showing me newer homes north of town, trying to duplicate the amenities in my current home, and still stay in my price range. I was thinking about calling Beth to see if she wanted to drive around the west end with me, when I hit something with the mower. I killed the engine and was head down butt up, when I heard someone whistle. I looked up to see John stopped in his truck.

"What's the matter? Lawn mower quit?" he asked.

"I think I've got one of the dogs chew toys twisted in the blades," I called back, feeling self-conscious in a bikini top and shorts.

John pulled in the drive and grabbed a wrench from his toolbox in the back of his truck. Within a few minutes, he extricated a knotted rope from the blades. "Here's your problem."

"Those dogs!" I said, disgusted. "Thank you for helping me. I don't know how I would have finished mowing this lawn."

"You look like you've had plenty of help," John said, referencing Mick.

I didn't know what to say. I was fidgeting with the mower trying to think of something witty but decided to go straight with the truth.

"Are you talking about my friend, Mick?" I asked, shading my eyes to look up at him.

"If that's the guy I've seen around here over the last months, then I guess I am," he answered.

"He's going through a divorce, too. A mutual friend gave him my e-mail, and we've been helping each other out."

"Hey, I get it. I've been there. I just didn't want to crowd you, when I saw him hanging around. Plus, I'm not into conflict. Don't misunderstand, though, I'd still like to go riding if you're up for it."

John's phone went off before I could answer, and he said, "I'll be right there." He looked at me and asked, "Ever seen a calf born?"

"No," I said, surprised.

"Do you want to? We'd have to go now, though."

"I need to put on some clothes, and I could meet you."

"You'll miss it then," he said, headed to his truck. "Come on. Show some adventure; you won't regret it."

I decided I wanted to see the calf born, so I jumped into his truck and headed to his farm. The instant I was alone in the truck with John, I could feel the electricity between us. It was hard looking at him without a mile-wide grin because he was so good-looking. John's strong, weathered hands gripped the gearshift, and we headed down to his farm. We ran from the truck into a barn, where we saw the cow lying in a stall with a bulge coming from under her tail. I was looking over a wood-planked wall down at momma, when it looked as if hooves were sticking out from under her tail. I realized I was in serious need of a cow anatomy lesson. I'm sure my eyes were the size of quarters, as I stood with my arms hitched over the stall, staring.

John went into full-on farmer mode. He took off his shirt and stuck his arm into the cow, up to his shoulder, and rearranged the calf. Momma was lying there mooing. John was tugging on the hooves, and the next thing I saw was the head of the calf. After that, he sat back on his heels and let momma do the rest. The calf slid out, and the placenta followed. The calf was covered in a membrane when momma starting cleaning her.

John joined me behind the wall of the stall, and we watched as momma cleaned the newborn calf. We watched the calf climb on her hind legs to move toward nursing.

I hadn't said a word since I left the truck.

"Well, what'd ya think?" John asked, covered in blood and cow fluids.

"It was amazing," I said with tears streaming down my face. "I don't know why I'm so emotional," I said, wiping tears from my face.

He threw his shirt at me to wipe my tears, and said, "My wife used to cry, too, every time an animal was born on this farm. I'm just used to it, and I know how wrong this can go sometimes, too. I guess I'm more worried about troubleshooting, than the 'miracle of life.'"

I was laughing at myself crying, making me cry louder. "I don't know why I'm crying; I'm really not a crybaby," I said, wiping my nose.

"Because you're a woman," he said, handing me a bottle of water and a paper towel. He walked over to the utility sink to wash while I pulled myself together. I had forgotten I wasn't wearing much, until John turned around, and I saw the look on his face.

"I'm a mess. I should probably head home; I didn't even lock my doors," I said.

"You couldn't look a mess if you tried, and I doubt if someone broke in with your dogs out front."

"True, no one wants the dogs jumping on their car."

"I could saddle up Missy and drop you back at your house if you want. She needs the exercise, and I could cop a free feel," he said, smiling.

I laughed at his directness. "Okay, that sounds like fun," I said, challenging him.

John yelled at Roy, the hired hand, to watch over momma and the new calf as he saddled Missy. He climbed into the saddle first and pulled me up, behind him. My legs were spread on each side of the horse and from that position each bounce from Missy caused me to rub against John's bare back. My arms were wrapped tightly around his muscular chest and abs. The fifteen minutes that I was rubbing and bouncing against John were intermingled with lustful thoughts and pure pleasure. The masculine smell of leather and outdoors escalated the sexual tension.

We rode around the farm first, and he was pointing out the different buildings and animals. We rode through the back pasture and followed the creek to my house.

"You feel like breaking into a gallop?" John asked as he kicked Missy into high gear.

"I think so," I said as we raced across the field. I felt like I might explode from the sexual energy between us. *I wonder if he is thinking what I am?*

"I'm going to let you off here, so your dogs don't spook Missy. You'll fall if she starts dancing around," John said, concerned.

"Okay, that's fine," I said, breathless, sliding off Missy under John's strong grip. I stepped away from John and Missy, trying unsuccessfully to contain my smile, and said, "Thanks for the ride . . . and asking me to see the birth . . . and for fixing my mower!" I said, realizing all that took place in under an hour.

"No problem; I was glad for the company," he said, grinning. He spotted the dogs running toward us and turned the reins to head back to his pasture. "Oh, and, by the way, your boob is hanging out!"

My mouth dropped as I covered myself. The ride had jostled everything I was wearing along with some hot and lustful feelings. He looked back, laughing, and I had to laugh, too.

*   *   *

I finished the mowing and then showered before I called Beth to see if she wanted to drive around the west end with me.

"Hi, Beth. It's Diane. Are you busy?"

"Not really. I was going to go for a walk. Do you want to come?" asked Beth hopefully.

"Well, I was calling to see if you wanted to drive around the west end with me," I suggested.

"How bout we *walk* around the west end? I know there are some houses for sale around here. One of them is adorable from the street. I'd love to go through it," Beth said excitedly.

"All right. I'll change and meet you at your house in thirty minutes," I said, feeling less energetic than I sounded.

When I pulled in Beth's drive she was sitting on her front porch dressed in running shorts and shoes, an oversized T-shirt with the logo from the country radio station, and a small, neon-green, nylon backpack. The backpack contained water bottles, a squirt gun with vinegar for menacing dogs, a cell phone, and a pen and paper.

"You ready?" Beth asked.

"Yeah, let's go," I said, feeling irritated we weren't driving. *Why can't I just say I want to drive without feeling I'll make someone mad if I don't do what they want?*

As we started walking, my moodiness quickly dissipated. The mature trees that lined the walks were in full bloom, and Beth was like a walking tour guide. She knew the style, age, and backgrounds of most of the homes along our walk since she had grown up in that area years ago. Beth had a real connection to the west end. She knew every detail of the park, walking trails, and the historic society's rules and regulations. When we passed houses with recent improvements, she would jot down the address if the repairs hadn't kept the historical integrity. She contributed to a fund that helped homeowners repair the homes to their original structure. She was going to send them a flier letting them know about the fund and their repairs.

While we walked, I told her all about my morning with John. She questioned my relationship status, and we debated whether I should mention the horseback ride to Mick. After a few miles, I had begun fretting about the long walk back, when we walked up on a pretty young blonde woman weeding her flowers, with a baby boy in the stroller next to her.

Beth started vibrating with energy, saying, "This is the house I was telling you about! The owner is here; let's ask if we can see the house."

"We can't just go up and ask her; we need to call," I said, feeling panic that Beth was going to drag me into a situation that I hadn't prepared myself for.

"Why not? She wants to sell her house, and we want to see it," Beth said defiantly.

"I'm all sweaty, and I wouldn't let some stranger around *my* baby," I said, equally defiant.

"Okay, let's just walk up and talk to her then," Beth negotiated calmly.

"Okay, but let's not tip her off if we really like the house," I said, fixing her with a stern look.

"Okay, I'll let *you* do the talking."

As we approached the house, we stopped in the driveway, and I asked the owner, "Excuse me, do you mind if we ask you some questions about the house?"

"Oh, sure, that's fine, I was just finishing," she said sweetly, as she pushed the sleeping baby toward us on the driveway. She walked over to the tube hanging on her For Sale By Owner sign and grabbed a fact sheet about the house. "Here are the basic details, but I'd be happy to answer any questions you have."

"Thank you," I said as I looked over the sheet.

Beth chimed in, thrusting her hand toward the owner, "Hi, I'm Beth, and this is my friend Diane. She just sold her house in the country, and she's the one who is really looking."

The owner looked at me and asked, "Is your name Diane Miller?"

I looked at her, shocked, and said hesitantly, "Yes."

She offered her hand, and said, "I'm Tanya Coles. My mother-in-law, Blanche, did all your window treatments."

What she didn't say was that she knew all the sordid details of my divorce and personal life.

"Oh, sure, I've heard all about you and Liam from Blanche. She is so proud of this little guy; she talked about him all the time."

"I was just going to put him down for a nap; you're welcome to come in and see the house if you like," Tanya said sincerely.

"Are you sure? I don't want to impose," I said. Beth gave me a dirty look for even suggesting that we might not go in.

"No, really, it's fine. Just wait here for a minute while I put him down and scoop up a few things. I'll be right back," she said politely, seeming happy to show us the house.

Beth was doing her happy dance. "I told you," she said gleefully.

"I know," I conceded. "But remember, be cool; I don't want her to know if I really like the house. It'll be harder to negotiate the price if they know I really want the house."

"Okay, I won't say anything," Beth promised.

I felt like I was standing on the front porch of a home straight out of a storybook when Tanya opened an arched top, sage-green door that had the original brass mail slot with the word MAIL imprinted on it. To my surprise, it was still used by the mailman. Above the door was a round window that stood out against the white painted brick. A colorful spray of flowers hung from the black coach lamp to the right of the door. To the left of the door was a side living room window with black shutters and a flower box, with red geraniums and ivy hanging from it.

As Tanya welcomed us into the entryway, I sucked a breath of excitement, as I stepped into the foyer and saw all the original light-colored wood floors with thick white woodwork and moldings. The small crystal chandelier hanging above my head was mirrored by an exquisite, larger version down the hall from us, in the dining room. To my right were two heavy, white, paneled doors with glass doorknobs. One was a walk-in closet, and the other was a gorgeous powder room. It felt like I had stepped back into a time when quality craftsmanship was dictated by elegance. The plaster walls were painted in neutral tones and in excellent condition.

"This wall color is the same color that I had wanted in my house, originally," I said, surprised.

As I peeked around the archway to my left, I saw an expansive living room with a large, ornate fireplace in the middle and a huge, floor-to-ceiling paned window, which overlooked the front flowerbed that Tanya had been tending earlier. In addition to the spectacular front window, natural light was streaming in from three other windows on the sides of the room. They were all topped with custom cornice boards that had the identical fabric that Blanche had used on the cornice boards in my great room.

I was so excited when I saw the fabric and realized I could use all my custom accessories that I blurted out, "Don't show this house to anyone else. I want it! Promise me, you won't show this to anyone else."

Beth laughed behind me and said, "Way to be cool, Diane."

Tanya was utterly taken aback and asked, "Do you want to see the rest of the house?"

"I'd love to," I said, trying to curb my excitement.

Tanya turned around to walk upstairs, when I squeezed Beth's hand, and she squeezed it back with a wink. An exquisite runner, with brass stair rods, covered the original wood staircase and opened to a white-spindled railing with a well-worn banister. My heart melted when I looked out the window at the top of the stairs into the neighbor's picture-perfect English garden.

When I walked into the master bedroom, across a squeaky floorboard, I was staggered by a mirror image of the living room below, equipped with the same magnificent, floor-to-ceiling front window and wood floors. My mouth dropped as I gazed at the cornice boards over the windows.

"These cornice boards are the *exact* fabric from *my* bedroom," I said, stunned.

I could hardly contain my enthusiasm as I visualized my custom bedding, chair, ottoman, and pillows in the room. His-and-hers walk-in closets were on each side of the door. I immediately started mentally separating my clothes from a spring and summer closet to a fall and winter closet. As I looked around the room, to my disappointment, there was no master bath.

The three bedrooms upstairs shared one large bathroom.

As we walked into the bathroom entryway, I opened a wide storage closet to the left and admired a wall of built-in cabinets to the right.

"This is the clothes chute and this is a dumbwaiter," said Tanya, pointing in the closet.

"Oh, my gosh, that's awesome," I said, fascinated.

I pictured my antique washstand under the round window that was reminiscent of a ship's wheel. The window had eight spokes extending from a small circle in the middle with two half-circle panes that spun completely around using a brass knob. Across from the window was a huge claw-foot tub and shower in mint condition. The bathroom was so luxuriously quaint that I dismissed my regret at no master bath. I peeked in the other two bedrooms.

"Anna will love this bigger room with the built-in window seat in the bay window overlooking the backyard," I said, lost in thought.

Back downstairs, we turned opposite the entryway into the dining room.

"I love the way the light floods through these French doors," I said as I looked out into the enclosed jalousie-windowed back porch. I peeked through a small window in the swinging door that opened into a large galley-styled kitchen with white cabinets that had pewter pulls and glass knobs.

Beth ran her hand over the massive gray and white marble-topped island that was centered in the middle with a hanging nickel pot rack overhead.

"I'd love to have this big island at my house," Beth said dreamily.

The kitchen also opened to the glassed-enclosed back porch, through another set of French doors. I could picture myself entertaining with the two sets of French doors open, creating a circular traffic pattern through the porch, kitchen, and dining room. When I peeked out the window over the sink, I was charmed by the view of the neighbor's pink and white climbing roses and ivy-laced lattice.

As we turned to the wall, opposite the kitchen French doors, we walked through a large walk-through pantry that led to a basement. I was pleasantly surprised as I stepped down into a generous family room.

Beth gasped, "I love these mahogany-paneled walls and thick moldings. And can't you just picture this heavy, stone fireplace at Christmas?"

I sat at the bar set in the nook under the stairs and said, "We can make good use of *this*."

Tanya walked into the hallway that led to the laundry area and pointed out a sizable bathroom, with a white tiled shower, toilet, and pedestal sink.

"This downstairs will make a comfortable guest suite," I said, thinking about when Ellen would come back to visit.

Just as I was fretting over a basement laundry room, I saw the laundry chute and the working dumbwaiter over the washing machine that originated in the upstairs bathroom closet. I felt like a little kid when I clicked the lever sending the dumbwaiter upstairs. Walking back upstairs, I noticed the alarm pad at the top of the basement stairs as we walked through the kitchen to the back porch.

I was already in love with the house and was ready to sign a contract, when we stepped outside. I was stunned to see a two-car garage, which was a rare find in old homes, but froze with amazement as I gazed past the garage. An old four-foot-high stone wall enclosed the entire area with towering trees that dripped with lavender wisteria and created a sweet-scented canopy over the entire backyard. A flat stone patio flowed away from the enclosed back porch to two long planter boxes overflowing with white impatiens and ivy. Descending from the patio and in between the long flowering planters were four wide stone steps that led to an enchanting sunken garden, reminiscent of a place and time long ago. As Beth and I stepped into the lush landscape, we sat on a bench in front of an ivy-covered trellis and marveled at the soft, green, grassy area that was meticulously surrounded with all my favorite flowers, and boulder-sized rocks that were between the stone wall and the grassy rectangle.

"This is breathtaking," Beth said, gazing around the sunken garden.

"Thank you. This was my husband's passion for the last year," said Tanya.

The hairs on the back of my neck and arms were standing straight up. I had goose bumps all over from my overwhelming emotions. I was ecstatic; it felt as if the whole house was beckoning to me, "Welcome home."

I gave Tanya a check for earnest money, with a contract to be worked out later with her husband, Bill. Beth and I, giddy with excitement, practically skipped back to her house.

There were countless details to sort out, from financing, home inspections, and closing dates, to telling Glenda I'd found a home that was listed For Sale By Owner.

"Let's celebrate!" cheered Beth, opening a bottle of wine. She hugged me and handed me a glass, toasting, "To new adventures." Beth was as excited as I was.

* * *

Later, when I pulled in the drive, Don was talking to Anna in the garage. It was odd to think that one year ago today, I would have simply stepped from the car and joined in the conversation. However, I sensed they felt as awkward as I did, so I greeted them and continued on inside the house.

Anna came in later and said, "What's for dinner?" She had been working in the hydroponics department six days a week at a factory in town and was making great money for the summer. My sister Anne's husband was able to secure a summer job for her in his lab.

"I don't know. What are you in the mood for?" I asked, wondering what she and Don had been talking about.

"I don't know. Can we just throw in a pizza?" she asked, sullen.

"That's fine with me. Is anybody coming over?" I asked.

"I don't know. I haven't talked to anybody yet. Did you know that Dad is living in Carol's house with her kids?" she asked disappointedly.

That was weird to think of him living in another home with another family.

"I hadn't thought about it, but I guess her kids are home from college."

Anna didn't say anything, and I decided to tell her about the house to prevent my temptation to bash on Don.

"I think I found a house today," I said cheerfully.

"Where?" Anna asked, surprised.

"It's in the west end, one block from the bike trail," I began.

We spent the next hour eating pizza and talking about the house. She wasn't happy at first to hear the dogs weren't coming with me, but she slowly warmed to the idea when I described the house. She acknowledged that she would be back at school, and the sole responsibility would be on me, so the decision was mine.

That night Anna was upstairs watching a movie with some girlfriends when Glenda called.

"Hello," I answered timidly, seeing her number on the caller ID.

"Hi, Diane, this is Glenda; I tried calling you today. I found some more listings for you to go see," she said cheerfully.

"Actually, I think I found a house today, Glenda. It's the house of the son of the gal who did my window treatments. They had it listed For Sale By Owner. I hope you're not mad."

I was braced for Glenda to be hurt and angry, but she wasn't.

"That's great. I'm kind of relieved, to tell you the truth. I've shown you everything that is listed on MLS; we were headed to the FSBO, For Sale By Owner, next. I'll be happy to help you negotiate the closing. I didn't have to spend much money toward marketing your house so, if you'd like, I'll write the contract for you, and we can do a back-to-back closing, in my office, from your house to your new one."

"Thank you, Glenda; I would really appreciate that. I'm sure the sellers will be grateful too. I'd like to write a contract as soon as possible. When could you go over there with me?" I asked.

"I'm pretty much open, as I had counted on us looking for houses this weekend. Why don't you call them and see when we can meet with them. First, we'll meet and write the contract, and then we can present it to them together," Glenda said, sounding pleased she could help.

At one thirty the next day, we met at the new house. First we toured the house. Anna loved it and was thrilled about being one block from the bike trail. After she left, Glenda and I presented the contract to the Coles. We settled on a price, set the closing date for July 15, and made the contract contingent upon a home inspection. She said she would let my buyer's real estate agent know that the addendum detailing my custom accessories was void.

*   *   *

Mick and I had e-mailed and taken his plane on a few trips over the last few months, but with Anna home and Don over packing the house, we hadn't seen much of each other lately. I decided to call him and ask if he would oversee the home inspection with me, which was scheduled the next day.

"I hear you bought a house," Mick answered, sounding impressed, and seeing my number on his caller ID.

"I did, how did you know?" I asked, curious.

"I have my ways. I told you that I kept tabs on you," he joked evasively.

"Well, that's kind of why I'm calling. I was hoping you could come with me for the home inspection tomorrow," I said hopefully.

"What time is the inspection?" he asked.

"I told the inspector I'd meet him at eight o'clock," I said apologetically, knowing I was asking Mick to take off work.

"I should be able to do that; actually, that will work out well for me because I need to do some maintenance on my airplane. I have someone coming by to look at it on Saturday. I've decided I'm going to sell it."

"You're positioning yourself to move to DC, aren't you?" I asked, disappointed.

Let's just say that with the new restrictions from 9/11 and my ex trying to use the plane as a weapon against me in this divorce, if someone is willing to pay a decent price, I'll sell it," he said, frustrated. "Regardless, I'll meet you in the morning at eight o'clock. I need to finish a few things this afternoon to clear my day for tomorrow. So I'll see you in the morning."

I gave him directions to the house and said, "Okay, thanks Mick. I'll see you tomorrow."

* * *

I was sorry to hear he was selling the twin-engine Seneca. We'd taken some memorable trips in it over the last few months. One weekend, we sneaked off to Niagara Falls. It was my first experience, flying in a small plane, sitting in the right-hand copilot seat. We had flown up to the New York side of the falls and rented a car, had dinner and flown back. It was a long trip, but the experience and views were breathtaking. Other times, we had flown into Meigs Field, next to Soldier Field in Chicago, before Mayor Daley had it demolished in the middle of the night, to go to a show or catch a game. Once, we saw Oprah stepping out of the private plane next to us.

* * *

The next morning, Bill Johnson, the home inspector; Mick; and I all met at the new house. Tanya had taken Liam to her mother's for the day so we could do the inspection. In the beginning, I followed Bill and Mick around, attentive to any potential problems. General impressions were favorable, and

I was bored pretending to keep up my end of a conversation about wiring, plumbing, and house codes. As long as they were impressed with the mechanics of the house, I was happy. I was wandering on my own, mentally placing furniture, when Bill and Mick called out for me to come upstairs. They were in one of the walk-in closets in the master bedroom.

"Look at this," Mick said, pointing at the shelves.

I looked at the shelves that angled out from the wall in the back of the closet. The top shelves were narrow, but as they descended, they became wider, with hinged treads that opened for storage, like a set of stairs. Tanya was using them for shoes. Mick and Bill had moved several pairs to the floor.

"That's cool," I said. "I could use the insides of these shelves for my secret hiding place."

Bill said, "Look up, do you see the attic access?"

"I thought we already saw the attic from the other bedroom," I said, unenthusiastic to go back up in the cobwebbed attic again.

"This is different; those shelves double as stairs. Take a peek," Mick said, smiling as if he was waiting for me to unwrap a present.

I felt the dread of spiders dropping in my hair at the thought of going back to the attic. The way Bill and Mick were grinning at me, though, curiosity won out. I used the stair/shelves to push open a trap-like door in the ceiling. I had to give the door a sturdy push, because the rubbery seal around the door created an almost vacuum-like seal. The door was hinged and was attached to a pull string that turned on an overhead light as it opened. There was a little room, maybe eight by ten feet or so.

"What is this?" I asked, curious with anticipation.

"I'm guessing it was used as a type of humidor," offered Bill, as he pointed around the room. "The floor, walls, and ceiling are made from Spanish cedar."

"What do you think these built-in boxes along the walls were used for?" I asked.

"Could be used for seating or storage," said Mick.

Above one of the benches was a little rack with a dozen little holes, almost like a pool cue rack. There was an old leather wingback chair, covered by a sheet, in the corner. Next to the chair was a little table with a brass lamp.

"There is no way this chair fit through the trapdoor, so this room must have been built around it," I said, intrigued.

"These Spanish cedar walls are all tongue and groove. And these boxes are constructed with cedar pegs instead of nails. If you look inside these benches, this round brass instrument is an analog hygrometer that's used to measure humidity. This copper line allows moisture, and this vent controls the temperature," he animatedly explained.

As Bill and Mick were impressing each other with their knowledge of humidors and the ventilation system of the little room, I started feeling claustrophobic and climbed back down the stairs. I was wondering if the current owners even knew it was there. I thought it could be my own safe room, in case of an emergency.

Bill gave the house a clean bill of health, with the exception of the roof, which would need attention over the next five years. I was satisfied with the inspections and felt pleased with my new purchase. I tried to take Mick to lunch, but he insisted he needed to work on his plane.

I was so wound up from seeing the house and finding the little room that I decided to call Beth to see if she could have lunch. I knew she would love hearing the story about the room.

"Hello, this is Beth," she answered professionally.

"Hi, Beth. It's Diane. I was wondering if you could meet for lunch."

"I would, but I've been so bad with my calories lately that I brought a yogurt today and told myself that I was going to eat healthy starting today," Beth said with conviction.

"Okay, I understand. I really just wanted to tell you about the house inspection; I just left there," I said, disappointed she couldn't meet me for lunch.

"Did it go okay?" Beth asked timidly.

"Yeah, it went fine, except for the roof is reaching the end of its life, but that shouldn't be a problem for a few years. What I really wanted to tell you about is a secret room we found in the attic," I said, tantalizing her.

"Are you kidding me?" Beth said, stunned. Listening to her reaction made me feel like a little kid with a new toy.

"I want to hear all about it; screw the calories. Meet me around the corner at Laurie's coffee shop. She e-mailed me earlier that she'd made egg salad sandwiches for the special today, and they are my favorite."

"Okay, I can meet you there in ten minutes," I said, happy to tell someone about the house that would share my excitement.

"I'll be there," she squealed. "I can't wait to hear all about it."

CHAPTER 15

On July 14, the movers came and packed the moving truck. Since the kitchen and great room were basically intact, it was easy to stay overnight the last night. After the movers left, Anna and I showered and went into town for dinner. We had promised each other that, on moving day, we were only going to look forward. The hardest part was Jack and Jill. Don had found someone who had a house in the country and would take them both. They had left happy and barking in the back of his truck. I told Anna that we had the option to keep the dogs if we changed our minds later. That seemed to ease the pain of saying good-bye to the dogs.

The last night in the house, after we had come back from dinner, we were sitting in the great room watching the pond and talking. Anna and I had an overnight bag, a couple of towels, and an air mattress with blankets.

"It's quiet without any TV, but it's so peaceful," Anna said.

"I would sit here and look out these windows a lot, when you were away at school, and, even though I was alone, I really didn't feel lonely, when I watched all the little animals come out at night," I said truthfully.

"Are you going to miss this?" Anna asked.

"Nature is everywhere. How can I miss it? I adore the new backyard, and I'm really looking forward to decorating the new house," I said, trying to sound positive. I was missing the house before we even left, but I refused to speak those words, even to myself.

"It's late, and we have a big day tomorrow. Do you want the couch or the air mattress?" I asked.

"Let's both sleep on the air mattress; it's a queen size," she answered. I was relieved to hear her suggest that. I don't think either one of us wanted to be alone that night.

*   *   *

The next day felt like the first day of my new life. I woke with determined confidence that I was back in control. I left the house with no regrets, only the anticipation of new possibilities.

Mick agreed to drive the moving van over to the new house and back it in the drive for the movers. They were scheduled to meet us there at three thirty. I was finished with both closings by three o'clock and had the new keys to 235 Bradford Place, Springfield, Illinois.

As the movers starting bringing in boxes and furniture, I had put Anna on the second floor to supervise the furniture placement and make sure boxes were directed to the correct bedrooms. I stayed by the front door to direct the moving men to the correct floors. My mom and sisters were unpacking kitchen boxes, and Mick was circulating from the garage to the basement. Various others were coming and going, making it hard to keep track of who was in the house.

In the middle of all the chaos, my new neighbor from two doors down came over with a bottle of wine.

"Hey, I'm Linda Farmer," she said, extending her hand with a bottle of wine. "I'm so excited to have another woman my age movin' in. I've heard so much about ya, I feel like I know ya already."

She was divorced with three kids. She sold real estate and Mary Kay and was currently dating the man that lived in the house that separated our houses. Linda had a statuesque build with stylish blonde hair, perfectly manicured nails, and a hint of a southern accent.

"Thank you," I said. "That is so sweet of you. I'll have to call you when I get moved in, and we'll drink this wine. But if I don't get back in there, I'm liable to lose my free help!"

After we talked for a few more minutes, she said she understood and gave me her number to call when I was settled.

By seven o'clock, the truck was unpacked and furniture was setting in the correct rooms with endless boxes. We were setting up beds when the pizza arrived. It was such a treat, after living in the country, to call for pizza delivery. I ordered three large pizzas and set them on my living room coffee table. My coffee table had been a forty-eight-inch round oak table that had been cut down to a coffee-table. It fit perfectly with my eclectic style, and between the love seat, couch, and floor, it provided us a place to gather around and enjoy the pizza.

"*Pizza's here!*" I yelled to the house in general. From the different floors, Anna, Becky, Mom, Ellen, Anne, and Mick all came into the room. We were all talking and eating and appreciating the break, when Beth knocked on the door.

"Hey, come on in and have some pizza," I said, glad to see her.

"Okay, thanks, but I can't stand the wait any longer. I have to see 'the room.' I have fantasized about this room for three months," she laughed.

My mom and sisters chimed in, "What room?"

Before I had a chance to respond, Beth was leading the stampede up the stairs, and I pulled up the rear.

Mick had stayed downstairs and was finishing his beer while Beth was standing in the closet fielding guesses from her captive audience about the shelves. She had amazed them by revealing the shelves' storage space by lifting the hinged lids when I interrupted.

"Beth, it's *my* story to tell!"

"Okay, but I'm the first to see it!" she conceded.

Everyone was expecting a shelf lid to turn the wall into another room.

"If you notice, these shelves can be used as stairs," I explained.

Beth climbed the stairs and crawled through the little door, with Ellen, Anna, and Becky following her. They were opening the benches and exploring, when mom popped her head through and said, "Look at that pipe rack over by the chair. That's just like the rack my Uncle Ralph used to keep his collection of pipes on, when I was a little girl."

After a while everyone had left to finish the pizza, except Beth. She was sitting in the chair thinking, when the rest of us had headed back downstairs.

"Beth, we're leaving," I called to her.

"I'll be down in minute," she said contemplatively.

Back downstairs, the girls were postulating that the position of the room was extended over the bedroom's entrance and portions of both closets. They were formulating a plan for spiral stairs to open into a fabulous two-story, cedar-lined closet. Beth would be aghast if she heard their plans.

After my sisters and my mom had left, Mick and I were sitting at the kitchen island with a glass of wine.

"I sold the plane," Mick said cheerfully. "They paid more than I expected, so I was happy."

"Do you think you'll buy another one?" I asked.

"Not for a while." He paused and fidgeted with the wine charm on his glass, seeming hesitant to broach what was on his mind.

"The FBI may be calling you, so don't be surprised," Mick said tentatively.

"Why?" I asked, shocked.

"I didn't want to say anything, in case it didn't work out, but the position with the FBI that I applied for looks like a reality. I have to go through extensive background checks. Just about everyone I know will be interviewed, and then I would go through training in Quantico, Virginia, in the fall, if everything works out. My buddy, John Fuller, inherited his parents' house in Arlington, which is just across the river from DC. He will be in

Iraq, between six months to a year, with the FBI. He approached me when I was out there about the possibility of staying in that house and supervising repairs, along with watching his dog while he's gone. He doesn't owe anything on the house, but it needs considerable work. I looked at it when I was out there and told him that I'd help him with the house if things worked out. It would be a good deal for me. I'd be working at the Hoover Building in DC and wouldn't have to worry about parking, because the Metro is a short walk from his house and would drop me right next to the Hoover Building."

"Have you told the hospital?" I asked.

"No, you are the only person who knows, but I need to tell people before they receive a random call from the FBI. I'm not going to tell work until I pass the polygraph and have an official confirmation letter. Many issues still need my attention, so I'll be preoccupied most of the next few weeks with them."

"Wow, I'm happy for you, but I'm going to miss you," I said, reaching across for his hand.

"You can come out, when you need to escape the drama," he said, as he smiled back and took a sip of his wine.

CHAPTER 16

The next few days were like Christmas as I opened boxes of my favorite things that had been packed away for months. Finding new places for them and rearranging furniture occupied my sisters, Anna and me for days, until we were satisfied with the rooms.

A few days after Roger and Mary, my ex in-laws, had stopped by to see the house, Mary called to say she'd just passed a garage sale with a wicker set she thought I'd be interested in. I thanked her for the tip and copied the address. I decided to go have a look, since my back porch was empty.

When I spotted the furniture from the street, I made a beeline to the garage sale cashier because I knew I wanted it. It was the same set I had been drooling over in the Pottery Barn catalogue but didn't want to spend the nearly $3,000 they wanted.

"How much for the wicker set?" I asked, trying to rein in my exuberance at the find.

"Well, it was my aunt's; she probably spent a fortune for it. I'm cleaning out the house, since she died and left pretty much everything to my mom, who doesn't live around here."

"I'm sorry about your aunt. My name is Diane Miller. You look like you have your hands full today," I said, noticing her kids jumping on the wicker set of furniture that I wanted to buy.

"Jeremy, Joshua, get down from there," she yelled at her boys. "I'm Stephanie Borzak. They are going to drive me nuts today!"

she said, pulling the boys off the couch. We chitchatted a bit and realized her uncle had gone to school with me, and that we had several mutual friends.

"I just bought a house, after going through a divorce, so I need a few things," I said casually, trying to play on her sympathy. "Maybe we can help each other out here. What kind of deal would you give me if I bought the wicker sofa, loveseat, two chairs with their ottomans, coffee table, two end tables, the four bar stools, the three lamps, and that white painted bookcase?"

Her kids were nagging her for snacks and crying they were bored. She was trying to concentrate on the items I just rattled off. "Would $500 be okay?" Stephanie asked, distracted.

"I'd have to write a check for now, but I could bring back cash if you want," I said, knowing the cushions alone were over $500.

"That's okay. How are you going to get it all home?" she asked, letting me know she wasn't delivering.

"I'm going to call a friend," I said, wondering the same thing. I called Linda, my new neighbor, since she had a minivan and lived close by.

"Hello," answered Linda on the first ring.

"Hi, Linda, this is your new neighbor, Diane," I said sweetly.

"Hey, I'm so glad you called. I've been dyin' to come down and see the house."

"Well, that's kind of why I'm calling. I'm at a garage sale not far from you, and I've bought some furniture for my back porch and can't fit it all in my car. Is there any way you could help me out with your minivan?"

"Sure, where are ya?" Linda said readily.

"Great. I appreciate this so much; we'll have to christen my new furniture with your bottle of wine," I said to tantalize her. I quickly gave her the address and started packing my car.

When Linda pulled up ten minutes later, I had already loaded the lamps, cushions, two end tables, and coffee table into my car.

I was moving at the speed of light, before Stephanie changed her mind or the boys climbed back onto my white cushions.

"Hey, girl, where's this furniture?" Linda asked. She was wearing booty shorts with a skintight tank top and flip-flops. The two men who were browsing through the garage suddenly became interested in the driveway items.

"I still need to load this group here," I said, pointing to the rest of the furniture.

"That's gonna to be a tight fit; we may need some help," she said for the two men's benefit that couldn't take their eyes off her supersized breasts.

"You ladies need some help?" they asked eagerly.

Linda winked and said, "My perky Ds work like a charm."

I wasn't sure what she said, but the body language was pretty clear. Between the four of us, we were able to repack my car and trunk, fill her minivan, and, they actually rigged the bookcase onto her luggage rack. I couldn't believe we'd made it back to my house in one trip. We had unloaded my car and were lifting the surprisingly light bookcase off her van when Dale, the neighbor that lived in between our houses and who Linda was dating, whistled out of his family room window.

"I'm certainly enjoying the show," Dale said as he continued to sit in his window.

"Well, if you were any kind of a gentleman, you'd come down here and help us," Linda drawled.

"Sorry, just on my way out," he said, leaving. Dale was well dressed and looked as if he tanned all year round. He was tall, bald, and what could be referred to as a "metrosexual," because he had regular facials, manicures, and pedicures.

"You're an ass!" Linda countered playfully.

We tried pulling one of the chairs out of the van, but it wouldn't budge. It seemed like the more we pulled the more jammed we made the furniture. We tried every angle from the back of the van to the front but couldn't wiggle the furniture out of the van. After thirty minutes of trying unsuccessfully to remove the furniture, we started laughing at the situation, because we knew it had to come out, if it went in. We were in fits of laughter, when the mailman walked up.

"What are you girls trying to do?" he asked, amused.

"We're trying to remove this furniture from the van, but it's locked in place," I said.

He set his mailbag down and, in less than thirty seconds, had set a wicker chair and ottoman on the drive. He looked at us as if we were stupid. We looked at him, stunned, and broke into an all-out, pee-your-pants, hysterical fit of laughter.

Later, we were sitting in the new comfy wicker chairs, enjoying the beautiful view of the sunken garden, and drinking wine. We were rearranging the bookshelves and deciding on which area rug looked best, when Linda looked at me and said, "Ya know, I can tell you're the type of friend who, when called, will help ya bury the body—no questions asked." She held her wine glass out and toasted, "Here's to my new best friend."

"Thank you, I feel the same way," I said sincerely.

We had just polished off the bottle of wine when her oldest boy, Nathan, walked down to my house, seeing her van in my drive and hearing us laughing from the sidewalk.

"Mom, Dad just dropped us off from the pool, and we're hungry," Nathan whined.

"Nathan, honey, this is Ms. Diane. She's our new neighbor," Linda said, in her mom voice.

"Hello, Ms. Diane. It's nice to meet you," Nathan said politely.

"This is Nathan, one of the three lil men in my life."

"Hello, Nathan. Did you have fun at the pool?" I asked.

"Yes, ma'am."

"Nathan, why don't ya order a pizza, and I'll be there in a few minutes, sweetie. Here's a twenty, in case it gets there before I do, and tell your brothers to put their wet swimsuits *over* the shower rod."

Linda had three boys, ages fifteen, thirteen, and eleven. She had been divorced for two years and seemed to have a turbulent relationship with her ex. She said she'd had a breast reduction right after her divorce and called her breasts her "perky Ds." Only she said it like a pet name, all one word, perkyDs. She said her husband, Luke, liked her watermelon-sized breasts and wouldn't hear of her reducing them when they were married. That was the first thing she did after the divorce, reduce the "watermelons to cantaloupes," and now they are her perkyDs. She told people she was five foot twelve, so she didn't have to say six feet. Her dad had been a six-foot-six Atlanta cop and had trained her to shoot and defend herself.

We visited a little while longer before we cooked up the idea that we needed to hang little white lights all through the trees and put them on a remote control from the porch. I was going to see how many lights I could find, and we were going to hang them as soon as I had the lights and extension cords. Linda left to go back to her house, and I wrote a list with lights, remote sensors, extension cords, and a patio set. I was thinking, *I need to remember to call Mary and thank her again for the tip on the furniture; maybe she could find a patio set.*

When Anna pulled in from work and walked in the back porch, she was delighted to see the completely decorated room. Throw blankets, candles, books, baskets, plants, and wine racks were placed on chairs, shelves, couches and tables, making the porch feel warm and inviting.

I wasn't sure if it was the wine or pure happiness I felt, when Anna plopped down on the couch, overlooking the view of the patio and sunken garden, tossed her purse and feet on the coffee table, and said, "This is awesome; it makes you never want to leave this spot."

We ate dinner on the porch and talked until her friends walked in a little later to go for a run on the bike trail. Anna ran upstairs to change, while Becky sat on the couch and said 'This is like a picture in a magazine; I bet you don't miss your old house now."

She was right. I loved the new house, and, when I thought of the country house, I remembered how much work it required and how isolated it was compared to the new house. I loved my independence and felt empowered to make my own decisions and begin my new life.

CHAPTER 17

The next afternoon I was dragging my cardboard boxes to the end of the drive for recycling pickup when Rose, the eighty-year-old lady who lived directly across from me, came out to introduce herself. Rose was five feet, if that, dyed brown hair with gray roots, and a distinctive gravelly voice from sixty-five years of smoking. She had a wobbly walk that made her breasts swing back and forth, making it hard not to notice she didn't wear a bra.

"Hello, my name is Rose. I live across the street. I've been watching all the moving and wanted to introduce myself."

"I'm Diane Miller; it's nice to meet you."

"Gotta minute? I'd like to see what you've done to the house," she said, more like an order than a suggestion.

"Sure, I'd love to show you, come on in," I said, amused. I'd heard about Rose from Linda so I knew she was a pretty obstinate octogenarian.

"You've had a lot of company for only being here less than a week. You married?" she continued drilling me.

"No, I'm divorced. I have a daughter who is a sophomore at SIU and a large family that, now that I'm in town, will probably drop over more."

She walked through the house seeming to approve. When we walked into the kitchen, she went to the opened French doors and looked out through the porch to the backyard. "Oh my, so this is what all the racket has been about the last year. That boy who lived here before you was passionate about this backyard. He worked on it all the time. This is the first time I've seen the finished product. It really is something to see. Reminds me of how formal gardens used to look." She sat down on the couch and proceeded to tell me about what the place looked like sixty years ago.

"Would you like something to drink?" I asked, thinking I'd make some tea, or I had Coke.

"You got any Crown Royal? I'd have a Crown 'n Coke." When Rose answers, it always sounds like a demand.

"I think I do." We walked into the kitchen and I set the Crown Royal and Coke on the marble island and grabbed a small tumbler for ice. "Do you want to mix it yourself?" I asked, not sure of the octane she preferred.

"You're fine, honey," she said, walking back to the couch. I poured a Coke for myself, knowing I had too much to do to start drinking whiskey that early.

She was telling me about Dorothy, the eighty-plus-year-old that lived beside her and across from Dale. She said that Dorothy had taught ballroom dancing in her basement for the last sixty-five years, and insinuated she was giving away a lot more than dance lessons to "those men." If that was true, I'd just gained a whole new respect for Dorothy. She drained her glass and went back into the kitchen for a refill. She was in the middle of another story when she finished her second glass and said, "You got any bigger glasses than this, 'cause all I'm gettin' is exercise."

I had to bite my lip from cracking up. I replenished her drink with a larger glass of Crown Royal and a splash of Coke. We walked out to the sunken garden, and I shared my project about the white lights. She commented it would look just like Tavern on the Green in New York City's Central Park. When I asked her about her visit there, she handed me the glass and said, "That's another story for another day," and wobbled back across the street to her house.

When Linda stopped by later, I told her about Rose. She threw her hands on her hips while giving me an exasperated look and said, "Girl, didn't your mama ever tell ya not to feed stray cats?" I laughed and asked her about Dorothy.

"Rose accused Dorothy of fooling around with her male dance partners. What do you think of that?" I asked.

"She has always said that crap about Dorothy. I think she forgets that they are both in their eighties when she says that. Dorothy is a very classy lady. She's a tall, thin woman with a dancer's body. She always wears her hair pinned back, with slacks and collared blouses unless she is teaching a class; then she wears all kinds of dance type costumes. For the fifteen years I've lived here, Rose has said things like that about Dorothy, and Dorothy refers to Rose as 'that busybody that sits in her window with a drink.' Once, Dorothy was giving me some relationship advice and told me, 'To your friends, no excuse is needed, and to your enemies, no excuse is ever good enough.' I just always assumed Dorothy had much more confidence than Rose; that's probably why Rose drinks so much."

"What about Carolyn, on the other side of me? What's her story?" I asked.

"She keeps to herself. She isn't there much. She goes to Florida in October and comes back here in April, and when she is here, I think, she stays with her gentleman friend. Someone keeps the lawn and gardens maintained and the snow shoveled, though."

"How long have you and Dale been dating?" I asked.

"That will take a bottle of wine and way more time than I have now to tell," she laughed. "The boys are goin' to their dad's in the mornin' for the weekend. I have to show houses tomorrow afternoon, and tomorrow evenin' I'm fixin' dinner for Dale, but other than that, I'm free on Sunday. I'll call you later."

"Okay. See ya."

Anna went for a run on the bike trail with her friend, Shelby, after work and was planning on going out later. I was working on the computer upstairs when it felt as if something was crawling in my hair. At first, I ran my hand over my head to feel if something was in my hair, and when I felt nothing, I continued working. The tingling sensation in my hair persisted until I went to the bathroom mirror, looked for any spiders, and brushed my hair thoroughly to eliminate that possibility. Back at the computer, it felt as if a hair was tickling my cheek. Since I'd just brushed my hair, I wiped at the stray hairs, but my cheeks felt smooth and hair-free. My phone was ringing, and the remote was downstairs. I made a mental note to vacuum the desk area, as I ran to locate the phone. The ringing stopped before I could find the phone. I went into the kitchen to check the caller ID; it was Linda. I continued looking for the phone when I heard tapping at my front door. I looked out the living room window that faces the porch to see Linda.

"Hey, I was just looking for my phone. What are you up to?"

"My ex took the boys early, so I have an entire Friday night free. Do ya want to do somethin'?"

"I'm just planning on staying in, but you are welcome to join me. We could open a bottle of wine; I have quite a wine collection from people bringing over housewarming gifts to see the house." I went into the kitchen to open a bottle, when Linda stopped in the dining room to look out the window facing Dale's house.

"Oh my! I never realized ya could see directly into Dale's family room from this window. I bet we gave the Coles quite a show on that couch. Dale never wears clothes when he's at home, which means he probably is sittin' naked watchin' TV most evenin's. I can't see that room from my side. My house looks into his kitchen, and I always see him standin' in his kitchen naked. I thought it was for my benefit, until Rose told me that she had seen him takin' his trash to the street at night stark naked! Can ya believe that? He is kind of strange. Do you know the balcony in front of his house? Well, it's directly off his master bedroom, and whenever he has sex, he hangs his comforter off the balcony. I call it his 'sex flag.'"

"Doesn't the man have shades?" I asked, feeling a little repulsed at having to see some naked guy watching TV.

"I have never known him to pull a shade in fifteen years, except the curtains in his bedroom," said Linda, dismayed.

"So why aren't you with 'naked guy' tonight?" I asked, smiling.

"He knew I had the boys, and he told me that he was goin' to some dinner at the university where he works."

A bit later, Anna was upstairs getting ready, and I was lighting candles in my fireplace, when Linda went to the kitchen to refill her glass and yelled, "*Turn off the lights! That son of a bitch!*"

I was running around turning off all the lights. Anna came running down the stairs to see what the commotion was about, and the three of us ended up at different windows watching Dale undress some woman on his couch in his family room. Linda was manning the dining room with a direct shot; I was watching from the closet window, and Anna looked on from the powder room. We traded views periodically, but the show was the same, just a different angle. Pretty soon, Anna's friends came over and were crowded into the powder room with her, also watching the show.

"She looks as if she is Anna's age!" I said, shocked.

"He'll lose his job if that's a student," Linda said, seething.

Becky said, "Why doesn't he turn off his lights?"

"To be fair, I'm usually on that couch, and I didn't have a clue that this house could see into his house so perfectly. Usually this house always had the shades pulled, and now I know why!" Linda admitted, embarrassed.

When Dale started stripping, too, Shelby started for the living room. "I don't want the memory of an old man doing it in my head; I'm out."

I agreed. When it was just about trying to find out who the girl was, I was willing to watch, but with Anna home and not finding Dale all that attractive, I left too. From that night on, Dale was referred to as the "Ugly Naked Guy," referencing episodes from the sitcom *Friends*.

Linda finished the bottle and went outside to look for a car in his driveway. She came back in mad as hell after recognizing the car.

"That girl is the daughter of a woman I carpool with to the boys' school! I don't even think she's legal age."

We schemed different scenarios she might execute later, but I was tired, and eventually she went home.

The next morning, I reached out for my paper and noticed it had only made it to the end of the drive, so I walked out in my robe to fetch the paper. As I reached the end of the drive, I noticed Rose and Linda with their heads together in Linda's driveway. Rose had on a flowered housedress that snapped down the front and blue terry cloth mule slippers with white plastic bottoms. Linda had on thin pajama shorts with a tight tank top, a flimsy robe, and flip-flops. I gave them a raised hand as a greeting and walked back into the house to have my coffee and read the paper on my back porch.

Ten minutes later, Linda burst through my back porch, causing me to spill coffee down my robe, and in a loud whisper said, "You are not goin' to believe what Rose just said to me!"

"What?" I asked, wiping coffee from my chin.

"Rose said, 'Linda, I saw you out last night,' when I went out to get my paper, because that damn paper boy isn't puttin' it on my front porch. There must be a substitute because normally they're really good about puttin' it on our front porch. Well, anyway, it kind of took me off guard, 'cause I couldn't figure out where Rose saw me till she said, 'You should have killed him.' I almost wet myself!"

"Linda, what are you talking about?" I said, frustrated.

"Okay, last night, when I left your house I waited till that lil bitch left, and then I knocked on Dale's door. He stepped out front, because he didn't want me to come in and see the evidence of his evening.

"I asked him, 'What are you doin' home so early?'

"He said, 'A friend of mine was at the dinner and wanted to leave early to have a drink, so I decided to leave early, too.'

"So then I asked him, 'So how old is your friend? 'Cause from where I was sittin', she didn't even look legal!'

"He actually said, 'She's legal; she's twenty-one!'

"*Can you believe him?*" Linda yelled. "Well, before I knew it, I let loose *years* of tae kwon do training on his ass, right in the front yard, and Rose must have been on her perch with a drink," Linda whispered loudly, with the look of a madwoman.

Anna walked out from the kitchen headed toward her car, when I asked her where she was going.

"It's Saturday, Mom. I'm going to work. And just so you know, I'm sure Dale can hear your whole conversation, because my window was cracked, and I did."

Linda glared over toward "Ugly Naked Guy's" house and said, "*That's right, asshole, and I can beat your ass again!*"

Anna and I looked at each other and burst out laughing. She went to work, and I offered Linda a cup of coffee. I was happy to focus on someone else's drama for a change.

CHAPTER 18

Linda left to go home because she was showing houses for the rest of the day. I closed my eyes and sank back into the cushions relishing the quiet and peacefulness of my sunken garden. I was lightly dozing when I caught a familiar scent. It touched on feelings of warmth and security. I was trying to decide if it was a tobacco or pipe smell. It was so comforting and was lulling me into a nap when I realized if I didn't get up, I'd spend my day snoozing on the porch.

I decided I needed some exercise, so I called Beth to see if she'd join me on the bike trail. Thirty minutes later, we were walking the bike trail when we ran into Cheryl and Jeanie. We all agreed to meet the following night at my house to drink wine and watch *Sex and the City*.

The next night, an hour before the show started, Anna was helping me make appetizers in the kitchen, when the girls started arriving. The first thing they wanted to see was the infamous room that Beth had already told them about. The room had lost its mystique for me. Beth showed them the room while I continued preparing the coffee table with glasses and snacks, and Anna lit the candles in the fireplace. The doorbell was ringing as the girls were coming back downstairs. It was Linda carrying a cute little bucket of vodka, ice, and shot glasses.

"Hi, Linda, come on in," I said, surprised but happy to see her. She would fit right in with the group. "Come on in, we're getting ready to watch *Sex and the City.*"

After I had made introductions, Linda said, "I came to celebrate with vodka shots. I made a five-figure commission today; that's why I didn't call last night. I've been negotiatin' the contract since yesterday and just finished an hour ago."

Pam said, "Congratulations! We need more shot glasses."

Anna ran upstairs for the shot glasses she had collected from different SIU bars, and Linda started entertaining the rest with her Friday night fight with "Ugly Naked Guy." Everyone was laughing, taking shots, and competing for the best story when the show started.

I felt more myself than I had since college. I was glad for the opportunity to show Anna the fun side of me that she would never have seen otherwise. In the beginning of the divorce, I felt so guilty for all the hurt we were causing Anna, but she had grown and had experienced so many of life's valuable lessons in the past year that I couldn't help but feel that if I had known half of what she does now, I wouldn't have been stuck in someone else's life for so long. I would have known who I was and experienced more of *my life.* As I looked around the room, I saw a wealth of beauty, knowledge, and experiences, and was proud to be hosting them.

After that night, Sunday nights became a regular routine with the girls and *Sex and the City.* Usually we would begin with Jeanie performing skin peels and the occasional Botox in the dining room before we adjourned to drinking and watching *Sex and the City* in the living room.

* * *

The first week in August, I was gearing up for Anna to return to school. She was going early, since she would be moving into an apartment and was going to apply for a job at the recreation center before the rush of college applications. If she was hired at the rec center, she had access to free workouts and lots of cute guys. Her dad had rented a U-Haul and packed her furniture from the storage unit. It was more convenient since Anna was living off campus and allowed to have a car. We each drove a car down with her clothes and personal effects. I had planned to stay the night to help with the apartment, and Don planned to return that same night with the U-Haul.

Two of her roommates, Becky and Holly, were already there when we arrived. Their boyfriends came over to help move in the furniture and left shortly after with the girls, giving Don, Anna, and me some time alone. I could tell Don felt awkward. I suggested we all go for an early dinner before Don headed out and then check out the rec center afterward. Anna looked at me with pleading eyes not to go, but I needed to prove, either to them or to myself, that we could have a civilized dinner together.

Don was dressed in spandex bike shorts and a T-shirt, so we opted for a local pizza joint. As we sat at the table, I looked across at Don. He was thin and fit. I could tell he was on a midlife journey of some sort that took him to places I simply didn't want to go. He was telling stories about hikes, books, bike rides, and foods that I just didn't want any part of. *If this were a first date, his interests would be a total turnoff.* I was in the middle of an epiphany when Anna asked, "What do you want on your pizza, Mom?"

"I don't care; you guys can decide," I said, realizing *I really didn't care. I didn't harbor any resentment toward him anymore.* I was happy that I had a fresh start at life again, and I wasn't going to waste it with bitter regrets about a divorce that provided me with independence to pursue the life I wanted. Listening to Don, I realized that we married before I knew who I was or what I wanted. I could forgive him the hurt he caused because he found someone who probably made him feel like he was a king. I had grown weary of pretending to participate in his interests and goals. Truth was, when he left it was like turning off white noise. I wanted us to be friends; I was tired of playing the victim.

Later, after Don left, we organized her things, went to the grocery store, and were talking before we drifted off to sleep. Anna asked, "Was dinner, with Dad earlier, weird for you?"

"No, if anything I feel weird, because it's not weird. I'm not mad anymore. After seeing and listening to him tonight, I realized we have completely different interests, values, and goals. I didn't learn who *I* was or what *I* wanted until after your dad left. You know, Anna, you should write down everything you truly want, so that you have a clear picture of what *you* want. Then when you meet new boys, you can compare them to your list. If I'd made a list of what I wanted and compared your dad to it when I had met him there probably wouldn't have been a second date, but, then again, I would have missed you."

"I know what you're saying, Mom. I get it," Anna said, drifting off to sleep.

The next morning we ran a few errands and went out for breakfast before I headed back to Springfield. On the way home, my mind was racing from making plans for my classroom to mentally rearranging the house. I decided to take a mental break and listen to some Enya, music I only enjoyed *alone*.

* * *

I was analyzing the epiphany I had about Don and was enjoying the peace and quiet of the house, when I heard the tap on the door that I'd come to recognize as Linda's.

"Come in; it's unlocked," I yelled from the kitchen island.

"I could be a serial killer, for all you knew," she said admonishingly when she realized I hadn't seen who was at the door.

"Serial killers don't knock that girly," I said in my defense, offering her a chocolate cookie from the package I was inhaling.

"So is Anna back at school?" she asked, stuffing the whole cookie in her mouth.

"Yip, and, no, I'm not depressed. I'm just enjoying being Diane without the mom hat."

131

"Shut up. I am so jealous right now," she said, taking a handful of cookies while popping another in her mouth.

"I know. No offense, but the thought of three boys, alone, with all those ball games and that testosterone would push me over the edge," I said seriously.

"Girl, you don't know the half of it," she said with a sigh.

"Well, I'm officially offering my house as your safe haven," I said, taking the cookies to the back porch. We sank into the sofa cushions, put our feet on the table and finished the cookies while we quietly enjoyed the view.

CHAPTER 19

That night, Mick called to check in and see how the weekend went at SIU. We talked for a while, catching up on the latest events of his move. He had received written confirmation on his position with the FBI. He had made plans to move to DC sometime before August 16, a week before my school started on the twenty-sixth. We had never defined our relationship. He still needed to settle his divorce, and we both recognized that we were enjoying our second round of independence, although it was understood we were monogamous.

Later, I was bent over unloading the dishwasher, when it felt as if someone pinched me on the butt. By reflex, I spun around, putting my hand on my butt, realizing the band on my underwear probably had been turned and snapped into place when I bent over. Feeling silly, I appreciated that I would be jumpy in a new house now that Anna was gone. I was tired from the long day when I went upstairs to get ready for bed. When I walked into the bathroom to wash my face, I noticed the round window was open and could smell a rich tobacco aroma from outside. Someone must have been smoking. I shut the window before sinking into bed to watch some TV. I was absorbed in a show when I thought I heard the now familiar squeak of the floorboard outside my bedroom door. My heart took a quick flip before I glanced at the doorway while muting the TV. I didn't hear anything. I knew I was tired and apprehensive about my first night alone in the new house, so I dismissed the sound to my imagination. I turned on the hall light, shut off the TV, said my prayers, and lapsed into a restless sleep.

* * *

The next few days, I had my two nieces, Emmy and Lizzy, and my nephew, Ethan, along with their dog, Bridget, with me while Ellen organized the movers at their house. They had sold the house and bought another one in Orange Beach, Alabama. The kids were having fun exploring my house, when I told them about my secret room. As they climbed the stairs to the cedar room, Bridget started growling up toward the door.

Emmy, said, "Bridget doesn't want us to leave her down there."

"It stinks like someone is smoking," said Ethan.

"That's not polite to say Ethan," scolded Lizzy.

Later, my parents and sister, Anne, came over or dinner to say their good-byes to Ellen and the kids. Mom and Anne were sitting at the kitchen island making a salad while I was layering the ingredients for a lasagna dinner. Dad was sitting on the back porch watching the kids play in the sunken garden. We were discussing Anna's apartment, when Ellen came to pick up the kids. She grabbed a bottle of wine from the wine rack on the hutch before plopping down next to Anne.

"Who is ready?" she asked, holding the bottle of red wine.

Mom, Anne, and I raised our hands, and Dad shouted from the porch, "I'm in!"

Anne poured everyone a glass and delivered Dad's glass to him on the porch. She sat back down, held up her glass, and said, "Here is to new beginnings." We all toasted to that!

After dinner, we all said our good-byes, promising to come and visit. *It seemed like one long series of good-byes.*

* * *

The following day, I was snoozing on the back porch, when I batted at something tickling my cheek. The warm air was commingled with the peace and quiet and the sweet fragrance of wisteria. It felt so relaxing to read and drift off. The heat from the cushions hugged me in a warm embrace. I was immersed in a pleasant daydream, when it felt as if a hand was softly petting my hair. I was listening to soft music playing in the distance and enjoying the comfortable presence of someone sitting next to me on the couch. I was aware of a familiar aroma, when the phone jarred me back to consciousness.

"Hello," I said, forgetting to look at the caller ID.

"Hey, Diane, it's Cheryl. What are you doing?"

"I was just reading a book relaxing on the back porch."

"I'm jealous. I never have time to read. The reason I was calling is to tell you several of us are going to Robbies for dinner tonight, and we were hoping you could join us."

"I'd love to. What time are you meeting?" I asked, looking forward to an evening out.

"We booked a table at seventy thirty, but we'll probably be in the bar area at seven."

I hung up the phone and went inside to find something to wear out for the night.

*   *   *

When I walked into Robbies, I spotted Cheryl at a high table. She popped up and gave me a quick hug, whispering, "Check out the hottie at the table over there."

When I casually looked over at the table, I saw John. He saw me at the same time and broke into a wide grin.

"Hey, if it isn't the flasher," he said, all smiles.

"Very funny," I said, walking over to his table. "How long were you going to let me stand there like that?" I asked admonishingly.

"Until I had to go," he answered with a smoldering grin.

I laughed as I saw a woman approach the table from the restroom. John introduced her as Robin. *Not girlfriend or friend.* The salacious look John gave me made me feel more and more naked with every word I babbled. I made polite chitchat and told *Robin* that it was nice to meet her. I returned John's grin and said, "It was good to see you again, John," as I walked back to the table. By then, Pam and Jeanie had joined the table. They were all ears, when I told them the story about the calf and the horse ride.

"I'd love to ride him," drooled Pam. I didn't really like hearing that.

Cheryl chimed in, "Did you see the look he was giving you, girl? I thought the air was going to combust between the two of you!"

So it wasn't my imagination.

I had a full mouth of food when John bent down and whispered in my ear as he left, "Looking forward to seeing the rest of you," as he gave my shoulder a squeeze. His squeeze was like an electrical charge. *I wondered if he felt it, too.* His words and touch caused me to choke. I covered my mouth with my napkin and said, through a choking cough, "You're terrible!" He laughed and walked out behind *Robin.*

After dinner and drinks at Robbies, we headed over to a martini bar. The music was loud, and I was laughing and having a good time on the dance floor before steering toward our table to finish my second chocolate martini. Once I sat on the bar stool, I knew I needed some fresh air and had to go home. None of us should have driven home that night, but I found my car and drove straight home.

I pulled in the garage and headed in through the back porch, locking doors behind me. I stumbled up the stairs, took off my clothes, and dropped into bed before hitting the remote to set the alarm. I was so tired; I didn't even wash my face before I went to bed.

I had passed out before my head hit the pillow and was absorbed in a sexy dream. I was in my bed, and the room was filled with the light aroma of sweet tobacco. I was becoming aroused by warm, skilled hands removing my panties. I could feel light soft kisses trailing down from my neck, over my breasts and past my navel. My thighs were parted and someone was nuzzling my . . .

BUZZ! BUZZ! BUZZ!

The next thing I knew for sure was that it was still dark, my alarm was screaming throughout the house, and the phone was ringing.

I fumbled with the phone and said, "Hello," realizing the pad to shut off the alarm was at the top of the basement stairs. My mind was in serious conflict with my gut instincts about walking downstairs. But the screeching alarm and the voice on the phone seemed to be guiding me toward shutting off the alarm.

"This is the dispatcher from your alarm company; our sensors show you have a breach in your system. Ma'am, we need your password."

"Password?" I asked in a panic.

"Yes, ma'am, we need to verify you are the owner."

"Umm . . . it's a . . . MY DOG . . . it's . . . uhh . . . JACK! . . . *It's Jack!*" I screamed over the alarm buzzing in the background.

"Ma'am, do you need us to call the police?"

Shit! Police?

BUZZ! BUZZ! BUZZ!

The adrenaline was racing through my body, making it impossible to think. I decided to shut off the alarm while I had the security of the voice on the phone that would call the police if something happened to me.

"Hang on a minute!" I said to the dispatcher, trying to gain my composure.

When I reached the first floor, I realized I didn't have a stitch of clothing on! I was torn between running back up the stairs for my robe or turning the corner through the kitchen and shutting off the alarm. I decided to go forward with shutting off the alarm.

I was just pushing open the swinging kitchen door, when I asked the dispatcher, "Does it show why the alarm is going off?"

"Yes, ma'am. It shows a breach at the kitchen door," the dispatcher said apprehensively.

I nearly froze with fear from those words, but I was inches from the alarm pad, so I willed my feet to keep moving. My fingers were shaking so badly that I couldn't punch in the correct code. I wasn't even sure I could remember the correct code. I was standing there naked, punching madly at the alarm pad, when all of a sudden the alarm stopped screeching, and my phone went dead. My first thought was *I'm naked, and somebody just cut my phone line.* I was seriously freaking out, when the phone rang, and I screamed. I jumped up and lost my balance on the stairs. I felt myself starting to tumble and instinctively grabbed on to something, maybe the woodwork; although, it felt like something grabbed me in all the confusion. I was able to balance myself before almost tumbling down the basement stairs. The phone had flown out of my hands and was still ringing.

I found the phone and answered, "Hello," sounding breathless.

"Ma'am, do you need us to call the police?" repeated the dispatcher.

"The phone went dead!" I said, nearly hysterical and close to tears.

"That's because when you shut off the alarm, it disconnects the phone line; that's perfectly normal, ma'am," the dispatcher said in a calm monotone. "Are you all right? Do you need the police?" the dispatcher asked again.

"Just stay on the phone with me while I check this out. I'm going to check the doors," I said bravely.

I could see the kitchen French door was slightly ajar, as if I hadn't closed it properly. I continued out onto the porch and checked the back porch door; it was locked.

"I must not have closed the kitchen door all the way. This is an old house, and sometimes a door will pop open if it isn't pulled securely. I'll just take a look around a minute while you are still on the phone," I said as I turned on lights, covered by a dishtowel from the kitchen. I decided to leave them on as I walked back upstairs.

I was feeling much more calm and sober when I told the dispatcher, "I don't see any need to call the police; I'll be more careful next time, when I shut that door," I said apologetically.

"Okay, ma'am. I'm glad everything was okay."

"Thank you," I said, wide-awake.

I went back to my room. Grabbing my underwear from the bottom of the bed, I remembered the dream I had before the alarm went off. *What the hell!? Was I dreaming about John?*

I went into the bathroom to wash my face and brush my teeth. I put on some pajamas and started to feel sleepy again. I climbed back into bed leaving on all the lights. After what seemed like minutes, I was awakened by the sunlight streaming through the window. I walked downstairs to make coffee, turning off the blazing lights as I went. I plopped down at the kitchen island with my head in my hands and thought, *I need aspirin.*

* * *

I was reminiscing over last night's events, as I reached out for the paper. "Ugly Naked Guy" was talking to Linda in the drive. *That's interesting.* I looked up from grabbing the paper, and they were both walking my way. *Oh crap!* I thought. *I really don't need this now.*

"Hey, guys," I greeted them, glad to have pajama pants, shirt, and robe on.

"Dale was just telling me that your alarm went off last night!" Linda said, visibly upset. "What happened?"

"If you heard my alarm, why didn't you acknowledge with some support, then?" I asked, agitated.

"What, and miss the show?" he said, amused.

I narrowed my eyes, knowing exactly what he was saying.

"It would have been nice to know someone had my back by at least turning on his porch light if he heard an alarm," I said, perturbed.

Linda pierced him with a hateful look and asked him, "Have you had any more babysitting jobs lately, Dale? Or as you refer to them, BJs."

Dale's mouth twisted in a humorous smile, but he didn't respond. Linda followed me back into my house, and we grabbed a cup of coffee and headed out to the back porch. I relayed the events the best I could remember, excluding the part that involved an erotic dream. We were laughing at the absurdity of it all, and I was able to put my trepidation about last night behind me. Linda had to go home, so she could drag her boys to church.

"What are you going to do later today?" Linda asked.

"I bought lights to put in the trees. I even have a wireless remote control extension cord, which I can turn on and off from inside the house. Do you think your boys would want to make some money this afternoon and help me string lights through the trees? I was hoping to finish today, so we could sit out here for drinks before *Sex and the City* tonight."

"They would love it. They'll be like little monkeys in your trees. I'll call you when we get back from church, but you can plan on us," she said, pleased with the idea of having something to occupy the boys for the day.

I felt energized, with a sense of purpose, and let go of the disquieting incidents from last night. I went upstairs to shower and dress. When I stepped under the water and added shampoo to my hair, the shower pressure felt like a head and body massage. My muscles were responding to the gentle kneading from the warm water. My headache was gone, and my neck and shoulders felt as if I'd just had a massage. Stepping out of the shower, I noticed the round window was open, and I could smell the scent of tobacco. I closed the window and finished dressing. I was in the backyard sorting out lights, extension cords, and ladders, when Anna called to catch up.

*   *   *

I was pleased to hear the apartment was working out well. She was hired for a front desk position at the rec center and was able to schedule most of her classes in the mornings. Since she hadn't picked a major, I had insisted she start taking classes toward a teaching degree. I wanted her to walk out with a degree that would give her a career. I didn't care if she didn't want to teach. If she wanted to do something else, that was fine, but she would be there an extra year if she didn't focus on a specific degree now. She had reluctantly consented. I didn't want to argue about classes again, so I steered the conversation to boys to avoid any conflict. She said she had met someone, and that he met some of "the criteria." I reminded her not to settle before we said our good-byes. She agreed; she understood.

*   *   *

After a while, the boys and Linda were over, and we transformed the backyard into a magical fairyland of shimmering lights. With the breeze blowing through the trees, the lights seemed to come to life.

Later that evening, I directed everyone to enter through the back. Jeanie was the first to arrive. I stepped from the back onto the drive to greet her.

"Hi, Jeanie, I set up happy hour back here tonight," I said, anticipating her reaction.

"Okay, I made this new dip, I hope . . . oh my gosh, this feels like I just walked into a fairy tale."

The enchanted ambiance that the lights had created elicited the desired response, based on the gasps of amazement from Jeanie and the rest of the girls. We spent happy hour overlooking the garden under the lights.

When Linda walked over from her house, she asked, "Well, did ya tell them all that ya went streakin' last night?" That stole their attention.

I retold the events of the alarm going off from the night before. We were all laughing hysterically at the embellished events from the previous night. We eventually made our way to the living room and settled into our Sunday night routine with *Sex and the City*, only *I* didn't drink.

CHAPTER 20

I had become accustomed to the tickling sensations on my cheeks and hair. There was a familiar pattern to them—first, a slight aroma of rich tobacco, then a caress to my cheek, and then to my hair. The sensation could be compared to a spiderweb that touches your skin in the dark; you never see it, only feel it. Although, instead of the creepy feeling of a spiderweb, it was very reassuring. It left me feeling comforted.

Tuesday afternoon, I was lying in my bed taking a nap when the line between consciousness and sleep was blurred by a dream. I felt completely tranquil. The aroma with a hint of rich tobacco lingered in the air. I was aware of pleasure enveloping my senses; it was sensual emerging toward sexual. I was relaxed in a dream enjoying the tantalizing sexual journey. Feather-light touches, flickering over my sensitive skin, were igniting delicious tingles throughout every nerve ending of my being. I had lost the ability to focus on anything but the warm, caressing movements. I felt as if a weight had parted my thighs, and my back arched in anticipation. My muscles were trembling with sexual tension, adrenaline was surging through my veins, until it peaked and blossomed into a release. I awoke breathless and fully alert, trying to process what had just happened. Trying to shake the dream, I sprang out of bed and walked over to the front window. I was staring down at the flowerbeds trying to remember my dream. It seemed so real. *What the hell was that? What did I eat? What was*

I watching on TV before I fell asleep? Am I losing my mind? Maybe I just need to get laid—although, I think I just did!

* * *

Later that same week, Linda called.

"Hello, Linda," I said, looking at the caller ID.

"Hey, Rose says you're holdin' out on me," Linda teased.

"What am I holding out on you about?" I asked, amused that I was the subject of Rose's gossip that week.

"She asked me who the tall dark-haired man was who has been hangin' out at your house."

"What? Does she mean Mick?" *He doesn't have dark hair.*

"She said she saw him in your bedroom," Linda said, feigning shock.

"When did she see this man?" I asked, feeling a little worried that someone might actually have been in my house.

"She named Tuesday afternoon, specifically, but other times were more vague," she said with a laugh.

My stomach flipped; I remembered exactly what happened Tuesday afternoon. *That was my "nap."*

"Was she drinking when she said that?" I asked, trying to mask the uneasiness I felt.

"I don't think so, but she's always convinced someone is involved in an illicit affair. She's probably tryin' to live vicariously through her wishful thinkin', since she isn't gettin' any."

We talked for a bit longer, and I knew she didn't give any credence to what Rose had said. I made a mental note to ask Rose more about the man she saw in my bedroom.

* * *

The next day I was walking the bike trail with Beth, who had taken the afternoon off.

"Do you believe in ghosts?" I asked her, curious.

"Why do you ask?" she asked seriously.

"Sometimes I think I sense a benevolent presence in the house," I said cautiously.

"I can understand that," she said, and hesitated.

"Does that mean you believe in ghosts?" I repeated.

"Why do you think I have dog treats?" she asked, seeking a serious answer.

"I assume to feed dogs. Why?" I asked, clueless.

"You can't tell anyone this story I'm about to tell you, agreed?" Beth asked.

"Okay."

"After I moved into my house I had this 'encounter' with a dog. Only . . . I couldn't see the dog. When I came home from work, I would experience a feeling of euphoria, like a dog feels when he sees you come in the door. The dog would lick my hand when he wanted my attention and would growl at strange men who came to the door. He made me feel secure. I set out treats for him one day to see what would happen, and they began to disappear."

She paused and searched my face for my reaction.

"Can you see him?" I asked.

"Not like you think; more like in my mind's eye, kind of like you would imagine a blind man sees. I have a sense of size and his personality, but it's not as if I could tell you that I see him like I see you," she said, trying to articulate her feelings into words. "He greets me when I come home, and he lies on my bed at night. When someone comes over, I can sense right away if he likes them or not, and, as crazy as this sounds, I gauge my trust for strangers by him. I see him as a big shaggy mutt," she said affectionately.

"I completely understand," I blurted out. "I have a man in my house that makes me feel . . . protected. He has a rich tobacco scent about him, and I've had some very sexual thoughts or dreams . . . experiences, I guess you could say, with or about him," I said, uncomfortable but relieved to tell someone.

"If I were you, I wouldn't tell anyone. They will mock you and think you are crazy," Beth said cautiously.

"I know. My neighbor, Rose, has seen him in my house. She told Linda that I had a man in my bedroom. She described him as tall with dark hair. I can't tell you the number of times he has caressed my cheek or stroked my hair when I'm standing at the sink or sitting still. I feel so safe, though; it's not as if he's a scary ghost."

Beth looked at me seriously and said, "The first time I went up in his humidor, your secret room, I knew he was there. I felt a flirty-like spirit, and I could smell that scent you're talking about. I didn't say anything, because I didn't want to spook you or for you to think I was a lunatic," Beth explained. "That *is* weird that your neighbor has seen him. We should take a bunch of pictures and see if we can capture his image," Beth said, reveling at the idea.

"I really want to talk to Rose," I said. "Maybe you could come over, and we can ply her full of Crown Royal, and then start a conversation about the man she saw at my house. I'm so curious about what he looks like and who he is."

"Okay, and if we detect the tobacco, I'll casually snap some pictures around the room," agreed Beth.

We started hatching a plan to go on a ghost hunt. I felt saner after talking to Beth, even though everything we said seemed a little insane.

*   *   *

The Thursday night before Mick left for DC, he came over for dinner and to say good-bye. When I greeted him at the front door, he tripped on my front porch step.

"I saved the wine," laughed Mick as he caught his balance against the brick wall.

I laughed and immediately recognized the scent of tobacco in the air.

Mick uncorked the wine, and we grilled steaks on the patio outside under the lights. As we sat on my new patio set talking and enjoying the view of the sunken garden, a squirrel fell from a

146

tree limb at Mick's feet, making him spill his wine on his pants. The squirrel scurried off chattering, as if it had been Mick's fault, and we both laughed.

Mick commented, "I can smell that tobacco again. It's very pleasant, actually."

"I think one of my neighbors smokes," I said as a casual explanation.

Later, under the sheets, my eyes flew open as I questioned who I was in bed with. The scent of tobacco mixed with Polo Sport lingered on Mick, and it was as if his moves were from someone else's playbook. It was confusing and tantalizing at the same time.

Later, when Mick was getting ready to leave, he said, "Now that I'm not going to be here to chase the men away, you're going to have men calling you."

"How do you feel about that?" I asked.

"I'd like to think we'd be honest with each other. I don't want to lose you from my life, but I sense you have other pursuers waiting for me to leave. I don't know where this road is going to take me, and I recognize it would be selfish of me to expect you to wait for me," Mick said, seeking reassurance.

"I like the idea of honesty. We've both been lied to and know how that feels. Let's agree that if we meet someone that makes us want to end *our* relationship, we'll tell the other person."

Mick looked me in the eye and was direct when he asked, "Does that mean you would sleep with someone else?"

I think I already have, if we count my ghost!

"I think we should proceed with the 'golden rule' and treat each other as we would want to be treated," I said, crafting my reply to absolve myself from my ghost's "advances."

We had come to a mutual understanding, and I told him to drive safely, as I waved, and he pulled out of the drive. I closed the door and turned off the lights as I climbed the stairs to watch TV in bed. The tobacco aroma wafted into the room from the hallway, when I heard the familiar squeak of the floorboard signaling company. Instead of the panic I had experienced before,

I found it reassuring. I could feel the presence of him in my bed, as if he were stretched out next to me. I had begun to perceive his essence. It was as if, at times, our thoughts were connected. I could sense when he was with me, and at the moment, he exuded a peacefulness that settled over the room and left me sleepy. I turned the TV off, said good night to the room in general, and fell into a deep sleep.

The next morning, I felt completely rested. As I walked down the hall to the bathroom, the round window was slightly askew. I said good morning to the room and felt a positive energy as I went downstairs to make coffee. My ghost wasn't an obvious presence; instead, I had the feeling that someone was always there, just in another room. I started becoming more aware of him when people were over. Beth's comments about trusting others based on "her dog's reaction" had made perfect sense.

I thought about Rose and what she had told Linda. I was rehearsing my conversation with her in the mirror. It was an awkward situation; Beth and I planned to approach her when she had been drinking, but I was impatient to find out more about him, so I decided that I would go up to the cedar room and see if I could engage my ghost in conversation.

"I would like to call you by name. What is your name?" *Nothing.* I waited and looked around the room. "Did you use to live here?" *Nothing.* "Did you die in this house?" *Nothing.* "Do you have some connection with this house?" I had started feeling foolish by then and headed downstairs, when I saw the tip of a yellowed piece of paper protruding from underneath one of the benches. I slid the paper along the floor until it was clear of the bench and began reading an old receipt. I decided to call Beth.

"Hello, this is Beth," she answered professionally.

"Hey, Beth, it's Diane; I went up to the room and started asking questions to see if he would answer me, which he didn't, and found an old receipt," I said in one breath.

"Really? I could work you in at twelve thirty. I have a clear schedule after that," Beth continued in a professional voice.

"I'm sorry, Beth. I didn't think about you having a client. Can you meet me at my house around twelve thirty?" I asked apologetically.

"That will be fine; I'll see you then," Beth said as she hung up the phone.

I considered what I had for lunch and decided to run to the grocery store, since it was only ten o'clock. Before Beth had arrived, I was able to run my errands and finish chores around the house. I had made a salad and a tray of fresh fruit and vegetables, remembering that Beth was counting calories.

"That looks great!" Beth said appreciatively as she walked in from the back porch.

"Are you off for the afternoon?" I asked, hopeful.

"I'm off for the entire weekend," Beth said cheerfully. "Where is the receipt?"

I showed her the yellowed handwritten piece of paper that I'd found earlier.

The Springfield Tobacco Shop 9/9/27

Sailor's Blend-Aroma, one of the most important aspects of any smoking tobacco, is the paramount consideration in this blend of Golden Cavendish Tobacco. Everyone within smelling distance will love it. 4 oz./ $6.25

"It's not much to go on, but what do you think?" I asked Beth as she continued to study the receipt.

"I just have so many questions, because I *know* this paper wasn't there before. I would have seen it. I searched that room for clues countless times. What were you asking him?" Beth asked, curious.

"Just general questions about his name and if he'd lived in the house," I said, trying to remember.

"This is dated September 9, 1927. Okay, what we know for sure is that he was probably around twenty, is tall, and has dark hair. What year was this house built?" Beth asked in detective mode.

"I think 1928," I said. "We need to talk to Rose. She knows this house almost back to the beginning. She told me this was the first house built in the area, and beyond the stone fence, out back, was pasture. I think she said this house was about ten years old when her husband built their house."

"I wonder if the Springfield Tobacco Shop is still in business and if they built humidors back then," Beth asked, beginning the investigation.

"We need to check all that out," I said. "I was wondering something earlier about your 'dog.' If you could sense my ghost when you went up to the room, I was wondering if I had sensed your dog. I was reflecting back to the first time I saw your house. I loved it before I even walked in. I remember feeling joy as I stepped inside. Back then, I thought I had an instant attraction to the house, but after listening to you, the other day, I think I might have felt his presence, too. What do you think about the idea of a sixth sense?"

"I actually think everyone has a sixth sense, but they aren't open to accepting the idea," Beth said pensively. "I remember when you came over that night, too. The dog was happy when you came in the door and trailed you through the house most of the evening. He wanted a treat from you. He doesn't acknowledge many people like that, so when I felt him trying to engage you, I wondered if you could sense him, and I said something about my house's stories, to see your reaction."

"I remember your comment, because I wanted to hear the stories," I replied.

We exchanged ideas on the subject while we finished our lunch. I was putting the dishes in the sink, when that familiar aroma came into the kitchen with a light breeze from the open French doors. I stilled and looked at Beth for any recognition. She had the same expression I did.

"He's here, isn't he?" Beth whispered.

"I think so; it feels as if he is mocking us, or maybe amused," I said, trying to read the room.

"Are we both crazy?" Beth asked in all seriousness.

"I don't think so, because there are just too many coincidences." I answered, unsure.

"Okay," Beth began. "Let's set some parameters. Other than sharing future 'coincidences' with each other, we give ourselves this weekend to play Nancy Drew, and then we let it go. That way, this doesn't become an obsession for either of us. What do you say?"

"I think you're right. The more I pursue this, the less I accomplish, and I need to focus on school next week. He doesn't scare me. I'm able to discern when he is around. I need to manage his influence in my affairs better, though," I said, smiling to myself as I recognized the pun. "I think if I can find out more about him, I'll feel more in control," I said confidently.

"Knowledge is power," Beth responded. "Let's start by finding all the previous owners of the house. I'll do that while you check the tobacco shop to see how long they've been in business, and if they'd ever built a humidor in this house," Beth said, sounding like Nancy Drew.

"Then we need to speak to Rose, preferably a drunk Rose," I laughed, feigning a serious tone.

"I'm going to use the computer, and you call the tobacco shop," Beth said, running up the stairs to the computer.

A half hour later, I went upstairs to see what Beth had turned up. She used her resources with the historical society to search the origins of the house.

"So what'd ya find out?" I asked.

"There weren't that many owners. The house was built in 1927. Springfield had a population of four hundred. It looks as if there was a scattering of farms around here. Beyond your stone fence, it was all pasture when this house was built. It was intended for Jackson Bradford. That's why this street is named Bradford Place. But for some reason, he isn't listed as the original owner. James and Rebecca Ernshaw are the original owners on record. They moved into the house in 1928. They lived here until 1972. After them, it was Martin and Judith Anthony. They lived here until 1999, when the Coles bought it, and sold it to you in 2002. It also shows your garage used to be a carriage house," Beth recited. "What about you? What did you find out?" she asked.

"I found out that the Springfield Tobacco Shop was sold to Tobacco Direct in the 1990s. They weren't sure about any humidor rooms and couldn't tell me who owned the shop in 1927. Let's go back to this Jackson Bradford. That's a year's difference between when the house was built and when the first owners moved in. Also, that receipt is dated 1927," I said impatiently.

"It looks as if he was a farmer, based on these entries about Sangamon County plats of land. He farmed this entire area," she said, pointing to nearly the entire west end, "until the 1930s, and you can see the land is subdivided then. Looks like maybe the farm sold or something," said Beth.

"Let's see if we can find an obituary for Jackson; although, back then, they only listed the date and how they died, if that," I said.

"Hellooo, anybody home?" called Linda from downstairs.

"Up here," I called. "Open a bottle; we'll be right there. Beth's here, too."

"Okay. Hey, Beth," Linda called in reply.

"Hey, Linda," Beth said, looking at me, shaking her head not to tell Linda about our "investigation." I mouthed that I wasn't going to tell, and we walked downstairs.

Linda was at the kitchen island with a glass of chardonnay, when she asked, "What are you guys doing?"

"Oh, we were curious about why this street was called Bradford Place, and were fooling around on the computer to see what we could find," I answered, with the half-truth.

"I know it has somethin' to do with the guy who made a large endowment to Millikin University back in the late twenties. Dale had told me the story, once, about some guy named Jackson Bradford, whose painting is in the library at the university," said Linda.

Beth and I gave each other a knowing glance.

"My broker's dad, who would probably be ninety-five now, knew him way back when. He was tellin' me a story once at a Christmas party, that this Bradford guy, who was a real ladies' man, had built some home around here and had what he called a prohibition room built in the attic. He had it all set up for booze and tobacco, with ventilation and everything. They'd had big plans for the room while he was building the house. For some reason he didn't get married and, instead, sold the house and gave the money to the university," Linda said, bored with her story, as we heard a knock at the door.

Linda's son, Nick, was knocking at the door when I went to answer.

"Hello, Ms. Diane, is my mom here?" he asked politely, swatting a wasp.

"Yes, she is. Do you want to come in?" I asked, opening the door.

Linda set her wine in the sink and walked toward the front door.

"Mom, it's five o'clock; we need to go," Nick said impatiently.

"Sorry, honey. I'm ready. Where are your brothers?"

"In the car!" Nick said. "Nathan says you said he could drive!"

Linda gave us an "I'm in trouble" look and left for an evening of ball games. "I'll talk to ya tomorrow," she said on the way out.

The minute Linda was out of earshot, Beth said, "That makes perfect sense. Those benches were for booze, and that explains why the chair was up there. Let's go to the library. It's Friday night; it's open."

"I know, but I still want to talk to Rose, and we have a whole evening where Linda won't be around. Let's have her come over," I pleaded.

"How are you going to coax her over here?" asked Beth.

"All you have to do is walk out front, and she'll come out. I'll bet money, she's sitting in her window watching over the street right now," I said.

"Well, let's walk out front with our wine glasses, pretending to look at your flower garden, and see what happens."

"Okay, but let's use the back door, because there is a wasp nest in the front porch lamp that I need to knock down. They're getting aggressive when I open the door."

We were in a serious discussion about whether mums liked shade, when Rose popped into the conversation.

"Mums are lookin' good," Rose said, breaking into the conversation. "You know my mother used to boil them and make chrysanthemum tea when we were sick."

"You're kidding!" I said, interested. "What did it taste like?"

She looked at me as if I was slow and said, "Chrysanthemums."

Beth busted out laughing and told her that we were debating whether they liked shade or not. She said they were hardy and could take either, but the variety I had would produce more color in the sun.

"Would you like to join us on the porch for a drink, Rose?" I asked.

"Sure, that sounds great!" she said merrily.

"We're drinking wine, but I still have Crown Royal and Coke, if you'd prefer," I offered from the kitchen as she was sitting on the porch with Beth.

"That'd be fine; I'll have a Crown with a splash of Coke."

I grabbed a tall glass and filled it with ice cubes, a couple of shots of Crown Royal, and topped it with some Coke. It was the color of weak iced tea.

"Oh, that looks good!" Rose said with a smile.

Beth jumped in. "We were talking about the original owners of this house earlier. Did you know all the owners, Rose?"

Rose kind of gave her a sly smile and said, "I've lived here since 1937. Ernshaws were the first. Becca and I raised our kids together, and after they moved, the Anthonys bought it in the seventies. Judy and I were pretty close back then."

"Did Judy ever tell you any stories about the house?" I asked. Beth's eyebrows shot up.

"What kind of stories?" Rose asked, hardly able to contain her smile.

"Did she know about the cedar room above the master bedroom closet?" I asked, probing.

"She did. I don't think Martin knew, though. She used to hide things she bought from him up there, along with Christmas presents from the kids," she answered in a reminiscent voice.

Beth continued our investigation. "Linda said you saw a man over here. What did he look like?"

"Look, girls, I'm old. I'm not stupid. I told Linda that because, God love that lil darlin', but she's got a mouth as big as her heart. I knew she'd tell that to you the minute I shut my door. That was my way of finding out if you had seen *him*," she said as she sucked down the rest of her Crown Royal and held out the glass to me. "Honey, I'll have another one just like you made the first."

I burst out laughing as I took her glass back into the kitchen for a refill. I handed back her glass and said, "Okay, Rose, then tell me who is the guy in my house, and why can you see him?"

"Well, I'm not sure who he is, but I've seen him for years. I used to think Becca was having an affair, because I'd see him in that front bedroom window. She never said a word about him, though. I tried catching him over here. When I'd spot him, I'd go over to Becca's on the pretense of borrowing something, but she'd be busy with the kids out back. So I really don't think she was ever aware of him."

"What about Tanya? Do you think she knew?" I asked, completely enthralled in the conversation.

Rose shook her head with a questioning look and said, "I don't know about her. She never mentioned the room. I don't think they knew it was there. But she seemed awfully timid. And it didn't make sense to me why they moved from this house right after her husband finished this beautiful backyard. By the way, these lights are wonderful. You're a credit to this house."

"Thank you. Why do you say she was timid?" I prodded.

"Well, they were always outside. It was almost like she didn't want to be in the house. And . . . I don't think her husband wanted to move. I think it was her idea. I often wondered if she had seen *him* or if he spooked her. She wasn't very . . . outgoing. Her mother-in-law is the one who decorated the house; she just didn't seem attached to the house like young women usually are."

"Did you see him here when Tanya lived here?" Beth asked.

Rose stared out to the side trying to remember. "I'm not sure."

"Well, what about Judy, what did she say?" Beth asked.

"Judy and I were best friends. We thought a lot alike. You two remind me of her and me. I think, in the beginning, she thought that she'd lost her mind. She told me about him, because she was scared for her sanity. When I told her I understood, and that I'd seen him in the windows of the house, she started confiding in me about different occurrences. She said that she could feel him watching her. And that he would watch her taking baths . . . and she said she could always smell tobacco when he was near. He smoked a pipe. That was about it; she never told her husband. Her husband traveled a lot, so I think, maybe, that's why he was more pronounced with her, because she was alone a lot. But he never came around much when her husband was there. Their dog was always growling at him too. Other than that, I don't remember anyone, other than you, talking about him. It's probably because you're single, young, and pretty."

"Did Judy see him or just sense his presence?" I asked.

Rose crossed her arms, put her hand to her chin and rubbed it for a bit, trying to remember. "I'm not sure, now that you mention it. I don't think she did, because she'd always ask me what he looked like."

"Who do you think he is?" Beth asked.

"I don't know. Judy had fantasies of different men she thought it could be; I think she even put on peep shows for him," Rose said, laughing.

Beth looked at me, silently questioning if we should tell her who we think it is. I shrugged my shoulders.

"Rose, we found out today that a man by the name of Jackson Bradford was supposed to move into this house but never did. Do you know anything about that story?" asked Beth.

"I do remember something about that from Becca. Didn't he sell it and donate the money? Yeah, I think that's what happened. I'll tell you what; I have some friends who would know the answers to that. I'll give them a call and get back with you girls tomorrow. I need to get home; I've got bridge with the girls tonight," Rose said as she put her hand on the couch to support herself.

"Wait, one more question, and then you can go," I said, holding out my hand. "Why are you the only one who can see him?" I asked, burning with curiosity.

"I think I can see him because he doesn't know I'm looking. I saw him standing behind you the other day, when you were standing in the bedroom window, looking down at the flowers. I've seen him mostly in the windows. If you didn't know what you were looking at, you'd think it was a reflection of a tree in the window. Most people probably wouldn't notice, other than I've seen it for years and *know* what I'm looking at."

Beth was the first to say, "Rose, don't tell anyone about this, please. If Linda finds out, everyone will know, and we have to work in this town. No client would want me working on their finances if they think I'm crazy."

"That goes for me too, Rose. Parents are not going to want some crazy woman around their kids," I agreed.

"Don't worry about me, girls. I know where all the dead bodies are in this town, and I've never told a soul. This will be our secret. I'll talk to you tomorrow; you two can come over to my house and look at my mums in the afternoon," she said, smiling as she left.

"She knew what we were up to from the beginning," Beth said to me when Rose was gone.

"Yeah, she's dumb like a fox," I agreed. "Do you think she was serious about dead bodies?"

"I assumed it was a metaphor for secrets . . . but I wouldn't be surprised with Rose. Are you hungry?" Beth asked.

"I could eat," I said cautiously, knowing she was trying to keep her weight down.

"How does Mexican sound?" Beth asked.

"Great! I can't remember the last time I had Mexican. We can walk off the calories in the morning," I said, feeling joyful.

"Deal," Beth said, grabbing her keys.

*   *   *

The following day, after our morning walk, Beth and I decided to run to the university library to see the painting of Jackson Bradford. He was a tall man in a navy-blue naval officer's dress uniform. The uniform's sleeve had three gold stripes with a star on top. The white hat was covered in leaves with a crest in the middle. Above his breast pocket were numerous brightly colored service ribbons and the gold wings of a naval aviator. It was hard to tell how old he was or the color of his hair. The plaque under the painting read, "Commander Jackson Bradford, 1898–1942."

"The plaque would put him about forty-four when he died. So he was my age," I said, staring at the painting pensively. "I'm guessing he probably died in World War II, then."

"I wonder how he died. That would be an interesting story to pursue," Beth said eagerly, enjoying our game of Nancy Drew.

"I wonder if he was married," I said, thinking aloud.

"Do you think that's him?" Beth asked.

"I have no idea," I said. "I haven't really put a face on him; however, he is handsome."

I snapped a picture of the painting on our way out with my digital camera.

Later in the afternoon, Rose was out in her front yard. Beth and I moseyed over to "check out her mums."

"Hello, girls. I have some news for you," Rose said, glancing over toward Linda's house.

"What did you find out?" Beth said conspiratorially.

"Let's go sit down for a while," Rose said, motioning us to follow her.

We trailed behind Rose to the back of her house, and to my surprise, she had a lovely backyard and screened-in back porch. The edge of the yard was bordered with bursts of color from every flower that grew in that climate. A birdbath sat in the middle, and bird feeders hung from most of the trees. The back porch had two oversized wicker rockers with handcrafted quilts and throws hanging on them, and layers of paint from over the years. A long dark green wicker glider held two needlepoint pillows that said, "You're my best friend because you know too much about me," and, "Keep this kitchen clean. Eat out." There was a glass tea cart, next to the brick wall, filled with a variety of different liquor bottles, glasses, and golf trophies.

"This is beautiful," I said, picking up one of the quilts and looking out at the yard. I was dumbfounded at the serenity surrounding us. Rose was full of surprises.

"It should be. I've worked on it for sixty years." Pointing at the quilt in my hand, she said, "I won best in show for that quilt in the 1978 county fair."

Beth's mouth was still hanging open, when she said, "You have so many different interests."

"Nah, I've just lived a long time," Rose said as she was pulling out an old yearbook. "I called some of my girlfriends last night, and here's what we put together."

Rose pulled a folding card table to the middle of the room and laid out the book and then went inside to grab her reading glasses.

Beth whispered, "Look, 1926."

Rose came back out and said, "This is my friend's mother's yearbook. From what we could piece together after talking to her mom, a farmer by the name of Bradford sold off most of this land in the twenties, and his son built your house for his intended. See this picture here, Florence Lorton?"

"That looks like you, Diane!" Beth exclaimed.

"Well, she was high school sweethearts with this fella here," she said, pointing to another picture.

"Florence was being pressured to marry Jackson Bradford by her parents. Bradford had your house built for them. The story goes that she caught him with another girl in the house while it was being built and refused to marry him, since she really wanted someone else anyway. The marriage had been his parents' idea because they wanted to settle him down. Evidently, he was the adventurous type and liked trouble. His parents had given him the money and land to build the house as a bribe to marry Florence. From there the details were sketchy, but the end result was he sold the house and donated the money to the university before attending the Naval Academy."

I pulled my digital camera out of my pocket and showed Rose the picture of the painting from the library.

"Is this the man you see in my windows, Rose?" I asked eagerly.

Rose took the camera and sat back on the glider. She studied it for a while and said, "It could be. The height is the same, but this picture is so formal, with the hat on and all, it's hard to tell. Who is this?"

"That is Jackson Bradford," Beth said, sounding very pleased with herself.

"It would make sense if that were him," Rose conceded.

"But you don't think it is, do you?" I asked, disappointed.

"Now, I'm not saying that. I just can't tell. The man I see in your windows is in loose-fitting clothes; he has dark hair and is tall. They are both good-looking men," Rose said, trying to appease my disappointment.

Beth jumped in enthusiastically and said, "I think it's him. I think he sees Diane, and it reminds him of Florence. He probably never settled down from a life in the navy, and when he died, he came back to the house he built."

I asked both of them something that had me so puzzled, "Why do you think the three of us can 'experience,' for lack of a better word, the ghost?"

Rose sighed and said, "I think most people are so busy trying to control what's happening right in front of them that they miss the bigger picture going on around them. They are so caught up in mundane details—dirty diapers, cleaning the house, working on job promotions, worrying about what people think—that they can't just sit back and enjoy the show. When they are weighed down with all life's responsibilities, they mostly only ever see the flaws in life; they miss the beauty and the mysteries."

As I listened to Rose, I thought about how much time I poured into every detail of building and maintaining the country house. I really didn't sit down and "enjoy the show" until everyone left. From the minute I set eyes on Bradford Place, I saw the beauty and mystery Rose was talking about.

Beth said, "That's so true, Rose. I was so bogged down, between me trying to start a career and worrying about all the trouble my ex had hurled at me, that it wasn't until I bought my little house that I started to see the bigger picture around me," she said, and winked, making reference to her dog.

Rose poured a drink, offering us one, as well. She sat back with her Crown and Coke and said, "Well, he liked Judy, too."

"Yeah, but he didn't touch Judy!" Beth blurted out, cringing at what she had just said.

"What? Now this story is starting to interest me," Rose drawled with a big smile on her face, putting her feet up on the little wooden stepstool. She took a sip of her drink and stared expectantly at me.

I closed my eyes at the explanations I was going to have to endure. "I'll need more than a Coke, if I'm going to tell this story," I said, holding my glass out to Rose.

She bellowed out a hearty laugh and took my glass. "What it'll be?" she asked.

"I'll have a vodka and Sprite," I said, shooting a nasty look at Beth.

After being peppered with dozens of deeply intimate and personal questions, we all agreed that the conversation *never* happened. I told them both that if a word was ever repeated, I was going to say they were both drunken liars. Rose threw us out later that afternoon, so she could get ready for dinner with her girlfriends.

As we walked back across the street to my house, I said, "I had a great afternoon with Rose."

"Me, too!" said Beth, surprised. "Did you see the picture of her and her husband on the table in the kitchen?"

"No, I don't think so," I said, trying to picture her kitchen.

"Well, I did, and she was *hot* back then," Beth said with wide eyes. "With all those trophies, she probably could have been a pro golfer in a different era."

We both walked back across the street to my house with a whole new picture and respect for Rose.

*   *   *

Later that night, when I was lying in bed, I said to the room in general, "Jackson . . . are you there? I love this house you built. I would like to have a conversation with you. Is your name Jackson?" *Nothing.*

I fell asleep with a sense of peace.

CHAPTER 21

The next day, I decided to drive out to my new school and set up my classroom. When I found my room, I put my purse on the desk and sat down, looking at the boxes stacked all around me from my old classroom. It seemed like years ago that I had left Mayo, instead of a few months. Beside the mountain of boxes were desks stacked on top of each other, and on *my* desk was a half-inch-thick manual entitled "Rules and Procedures," with a sticky note that said, "Please read and sign before the students' first day of school."

I could hear other teachers in the halls and classrooms. I didn't know anyone there yet, although I'd met a few at the end of last school year during a consolidation meeting. I began the massive undertaking of reading the labels on boxes, sorting and arranging them by center areas, when the other fifth-grade teacher came in to introduce herself to me.

"Hey, want some help?" a young, pretty, brown-haired woman asked.

"I'd love some!" I responded without hesitating, realizing the *old* me would have said, *No, that's okay,* and tried to do it all myself.

"You must be Ms. Miller. I'm Heather Dennis; we'll be teaching together this year."

"It's nice to meet you, Heather. How long have you taught here?" I asked, in an effort to acquaint myself.

"I started here right after I married my husband, Jason, and with the exception of the year I took off when I had my daughter, Madison, I've been here seven years. Before that, I taught high school math."

"What made you switch to elementary?" I asked, curious.

"The joke was on me. I was tired of *their* attitudes!" We laughed, knowing fifth grade had plenty of attitude. "What about you? How long have you taught?" she asked.

"I taught the last eight years at Mayo, teaching fifth grade, and before that I sold real estate," I said.

"What made *you* switch careers?" she asked, surprised.

"I think, in the beginning, I thought the hours would be better for my family, and I also wanted to contribute toward bettering future generations. I guess I wanted to make a difference," I answered thoughtfully.

"I want to tell you something . . . and I hope you don't hold anything against me for it . . . but I wanted you to hear it from me first," Heather said. I could see the subject was difficult for her to broach.

"Okay," I said, bracing myself, sensing she wanted a response.

"My aunt is Carol Dutton. I think what she did was really shitty, and an embarrassment to our whole family," she spat out in one breath.

"Well, great minds think alike, then, 'cause I think what she did was shitty, and I was certainly humiliated by it," I said, smiling jovially.

I was trying to bring levity to the awkward situation. I was glad she told me, and I wanted us to become friends.

"Heather, I appreciate you telling me that. I don't hold anything against you, and I would encourage you not to worry about what I or anyone else thinks. What she did is a reflection on her, not you or your family. Granted the whole experience was painful, to say the least, but I have moved past it and am looking forward to starting over in a new school, setting up my new classroom, and making new friends," I said, giving her a genuine smile.

I could see the instant relief in Heather's eyes. She could sense my sincerity and said, "I'm so happy to hear you say that; I was afraid this might be really uncomfortable."

"Only if *you* let it be, because, to tell you the truth, I haven't thought about them in a long while," I said, realizing that since I moved to Bradford Place, I'd hardly given them a thought.

"Oh, good," she said with a sigh of relief. "I feel so much better. I'm looking forward to this year, too."

We continued our discussion about classrooms and curriculum while moving furniture and unpacking boxes.

*   *   *

Later that night, I was sitting on the floor in my living room making student name tags for the desks in my classroom. I was copying the names from my class list onto each laminated name tag and cutting magnetic tape for the back of each tag. They were organized into piles on the coffee table. I was tired from the long day at school, so I decided to brew a fresh pot of coffee, so that I could finish the project before I went to bed. I left the neat little piles on the table and went into the kitchen. When I sat down with my cup of coffee, ready to resume my project, I noticed some of the name tags had fallen to the floor. They had fallen in a straight line. I sat back on the couch and looked at the name tags for a minute, enjoying the hot coffee.

I know these were in organized piles when I left the room.

The names on the floor were Justin, Allison, Caitlyn, and Kyle. The tags were from different piles, because some had magnets and others didn't.

What are the odds of one name tag from each pile falling on the floor? Is that a mnemonic for Jack?

I spoke to the room, "Jack, did you knock my name tags to the floor to spell your name?" I could smell the tobacco aroma. Nothing happened so I continued sorting and finishing the tags, feeling his comforting presence. When I was finished, I stacked them all neatly in a pile and secured them with a rubber band before slipping them back into my schoolbag.

I had a second wind from the coffee, so I pulled a box of large manila envelopes from my bag and began the arduous task of gluing, collating, and compiling "Welcome to my classroom" packets. It was starting to get late when I finished labeling the names of each student on the envelopes. I stacked and placed them in the box and put them, along with my schoolbag, on the dining room table, turned off the lights, and went upstairs.

When I went into the bathroom, the window was slightly open, and I could smell the familiar aroma. I shut the window, washed my face, and thought I heard someone say, "Diane." I looked in the mirror behind me, and for a split second thought I caught a shadow of a reflection. I passed it off as me being tired and went to bed. Throughout the night, I kept waking up and having to pull up my covers that had drifted to the bottom of the bed.

The next morning, I woke to the sun streaming through the front window.

I can't believe I didn't shut that blind last night.

I lay there reviewing my mental list of tasks that I needed to get accomplished for the day, when I heard a familiar tap at my door. I looked at the clock by my bed, and it said six thirty. *Why is Linda at my house so early?*

I shut off the alarm remote, went downstairs, and opened the door.

"Hey, Diane. You up?" Linda asked, still in her robe.

"I am now. Do you want some coffee?" I asked, turning toward the kitchen.

Linda followed me to the kitchen and sat at the island. "I did a bad thing last night," she said, regretfully.

"What?" I asked, turning around to give her my full attention.

"Well . . . if you look outside, you'll see Dale's sex flag hanging."

She looked at me expectantly. I turned back around to grab some mugs while the coffee finished brewing. I didn't know what to say.

"Say it, I'm stupid. He's just using me," Linda said, admonishing herself.

"Do you think that's what I'm thinking?" I asked, surprised and a little insulted.

"Maybe I'm projecting my judgment into your thoughts," said Linda sadly.

"Honestly, Linda," I said, pouring the coffee, "I have decided to only depend on a man for intimacy, so maybe *you* should too."

She took the cup of coffee and sat quietly for a while. "That is really true. I don't need him to pay my bills or raise my boys . . . what else do I need him for?"

"Do you care about him?" I asked bluntly.

"He's convenient. And I suppose I'm convenient for him too."

"Linda, don't beat yourself up. Where are the boys?" I asked.

"They left last night with their dad. Since this is the last week before school starts, I told my ex he could take them during the week if he wanted. Dale saw them leave and hollered at me to share a glass of wine as a peace offering, and one thing led to another."

"Well, good. Now the animosity is gone, and you can just be friends . . . with benefits," I said, raising my brows, questioning.

"Do ya think I'm a whore?" Linda asked, smiling.

"Not unless you pimp yourself out for a measly bottle of wine," I said with one eyebrow raised. "Just act like nothing happened. Next time, you be the aggressor and let him know you are in control. And go out with someone else to show him that he is just a convenience for *you*."

"I'd like to say there won't be a next time," Linda said, trying to be remorseful.

I set my coffee down to use the restroom, and when I walked through the dining room, I noticed my schoolbag was knocked to the floor, and four envelopes were on the floor. Justin. Allison. Caitlyn. Kyle. *What are the odds? Well, hello, Jack.*

* * *

Later that morning, I was pulling out of my driveway when I noticed Linda's boys jumping out of their dad's car carrying a white Styrofoam bucket, as if they had gone fishing. I waved as I drove by and continued on to my classroom to organize desks with the tags and envelopes I had finished the night before. I arranged my front row with Justin, Allison, Caitlyn, and Kyle, smiling to myself. When I was satisfied with my room, I walked through the halls for a break, peeking into rooms and introducing myself to teachers I hadn't met.

Carrie Nichols taught fourth grade. When I introduced myself to her, she said, "So you are the famous Diane Miller."

"What do you mean?" I asked, puzzled.

"My brother-in-law is so in lust with you. He literally drove by your house every day, and this is a man that doesn't leave his farm to do his own grocery shopping, but he would find an excuse to drive by *your* house daily."

"Is John Nichols your brother-in-law?" I asked, surprised and flattered.

"Yeah. He thinks your ex is the biggest idiot on the face of the planet," she continued.

"I saw him the other night out with his girlfriend, Robin," I said, looking to find out who Robin was.

"That skank! She is *not* his girlfriend. Where did you see them?"

"At Robbies," I said, intrigued by her reaction.

"That hound dog! I can't believe he was sniffing around her again. He must have been horny."

I laughed at her directness. *It must run in the family.*

"What did he say about me?" I asked, curious.

"In the beginning, he was all pissed that you guys bought that property, because he was afraid you were going to subdivide the property behind his pastures. But when he saw your house go up, and the pond reconstructed, he settled down. He admired how you turned it into a park setting. He got real interested after your husband left. He even plowed your drive one day, and he won't even plow mine!"

So it was John who plowed my drive back then, not Don.

"I guess he saw you in the yard mowing and with your dogs. I know for sure you about gave him an orgasm one day when you were bent over a broken mower or something."

I burst out laughing at Carrie. *She didn't hold anything back!*

"The guys were all talking about how you came down to the barn in a bikini to watch one of the calves born."

"*I did not!* I had shorts and a bikini top on mowing, when he all but accosted me, to go down there. I tried to go in and put more clothes on, but he wouldn't give me a minute to go inside and grab a T-shirt."

Carrie was laughing and mocking me in fun. We were sharing stories, and she was giving me the whole scoop on John. I knew she'd go back and tell him every word I said, with added embellishments. I liked her. This school year was going to be fun.

Heather heard us and came over to see why we were laughing. Carrie told her that her brother-in-law had wet, nasty dreams about me, and we all cracked up again. Later, Heather asked if we could help her move some furniture, so I went to her room and helped her hang posters and move some heavier furniture before heading home for the day.

* * *

When I walked into the house, I "sensed a turbulence in the force." I looked around the house as if I'd been broken into . . . something felt off . . . angry. I grabbed a ball bat from the closet and walked through the house. I could smell the familiar aroma in the living room.

"Jack?" I waited for a reply of some kind. *Nothing.* I went through the house room by room; with the exception of the living room, everything else looked and felt peaceful. I went back to the kitchen and made a grilled chicken salad.

I was sitting on the back porch eating the salad, when Linda walked in.

"I need a place to hide out," she said anxiously as she dropped into the love seat across from me.

"Do you want something to drink?" I asked to be polite.

"No, thanks. This has been a crazy day. Everybody hates me; my boys have all been grounded to their rooms for the rest of their lives, and, frankly, I don't know what to do," Linda said, on the verge of tears.

"What's the matter?" I asked sympathetically.

Linda's voice cracked when she heaved a heavy sigh and said, "The boys came back from their dad's this mornin' and had a bucket full of frogs and two small garter snakes. They wanted to watch the snakes eat the frogs. I freaked when I saw what they had brought into the house. Damn my ex; you know he knew! Well, anyway, I told the boys to git rid of the bucket immediately. I thought they were goin' to the duck pond or the bike trail to let the snakes and frogs loose. I jumped in the shower while they were gone. The phone was ringin' before I stepped out of the shower. By the time I talked to the first neighbor, the boys had gone up and down the block puttin' the contents of the bucket through mail slots in the doors of our neighbors."

Adrenaline shot threw me as my eyes grew wide, and my heart started pounding. *"Did they put them in my house? Whose house got the snakes?"* I panicked.

"I don't think your house has any, because they were covered in wasp stings when they came home. They lied to me, at first, sayin' they didn't know I was in the shower and went to your house lookin' for me when wasps stung them. They are covered in bakin' soda and calamine lotion. If I wasn't so mad at my boys, I'd feel sorry for them," Linda said, throwing her hands in the air with tears streaming down her cheeks.

"I've been meaning to knock that down; it's just the nest is inside the lamp. I'll need to get some wasp spray," I said, remorseful.

"What am I gonna do with those boys? They think this whole thing is a joke . . . and my ex is probably laughin' his ass off encouraging 'em," Linda said, defeated.

The school teacher came out in me, when I told her, "To begin with, you need to make them apologize to every neighbor they did that to!" I demanded.

"They're lyin' to me; they keep sayin' they didn't do it," Linda said hopelessly.

"You tell them that they are going to be grounded a month for every neighbor who finds something in their house, whether they put it there or not. If they confess whose houses they set the frogs and snakes in, then they will get off with yard work for those neighbors. Regardless, I'd start with grounding them a month for every neighbor who has called," I said, ready to go after the boys myself.

Linda clarified. "Okay, so you're sayin' ground them for six months, let's say, up front. And if they tell the truth 'bout which houses they pranked, then make 'em apologize and do yard work for the neighbor, instead of the groundin'. Right?"

"Yeah, that way it forces the truth out of the boys and reduces *your* punishment because you'll be grounded too," I said sympathetically.

"Well, I think there were only two snakes and, apparently, they were found. They put them in the Schmidts and Snapps houses for retaliation over gettin' blamed last Halloween for some car windows bein' soaped—which I'm sure they did," Linda said, and rolled her eyes, exasperated.

"Have you talked to your ex about it?" I asked curious.

"No, he'll blame me; sayin' I wasn't watchin' 'em."

"That's bullshit!" I exploded. "He's the one who sent them home with the bucket in the first place! You call him and tell him that he is going to come over and sit down with you as a united front and settle this with those boys. They could probably be in legal trouble if someone wanted to push this; you need to be proactive," I insisted. "Here, call him now while I'm here for moral support," I said, handing her the phone. "Call him!"

Linda dialed the phone and said, "Hey, Luke, call me . . . oh, I was just leavin' a message. Well, the boys pranked the neighbors by puttin' that bucket of frogs and snakes you sent home with them through the mail slots of my neighbors."

Linda mouthed to me, "Asshole is laughin'. I told ya."

I held up my fist with a mean face and said, "Make him be a parent, and a united front with you!"

Linda sounded like she was scolding a child, when she said, "Look, Luke, this is serious. The neighbors are callin' the police and filin' charges for criminal damage. You need to git over here and sit down with me so they know we mean business. If I can get the boys to apologize and offer free yard work like rakin' leaves or somethin', then maybe we can keep this from goin' to court. Yeah, that works for me. Okay, I'll see ya in an hour."

Linda hung up the phone and gave me a high five. "Girl. That. Felt. Great!"

"A wise woman once told me, 'People treat you how you let them treat you,'" I said, thinking of Yolie.

"I'm goin' to call this cop I sold a house to and see if he'll come over and scare the crap out of all of 'em," Linda said, letting her newfound power take over.

"Do you think he'll do it?" I asked, proud of the way she was taking control.

"Only one way to find out," she said as she walked toward the door, ready to kick some ass. "Thanks for the pep talk, Diane. I'll let you know how it turns out," she said over her shoulder.

I walked into my foyer looking around for any signs of frogs. It appeared fine. "Thanks, Jack, for running off the boys today," I said aloud. "I'm assuming the anger I sensed earlier could be attributed to you and the frogs."

"Juvenile delinquents."

Did I just hear someone say juvenile delinquents?

"What? What did you say?" I asked in disbelief. *Nothing.*

I decided to get my schoolbag and rank reading levels in front of the TV. I had all the students' reading scores sorted into four reading groups with similar scores when the doorbell rang. I looked out the window and saw Beth.

"Hey, come in," I said, opening the door. "What are you doing?"

"I walked over wondering if you wanted to walk," Beth said.

"Why didn't you call? I would have met you," I asked.

"I just started walking and didn't realize I would end up here," Beth said. She seemed quiet, like she'd had a stressful day.

"Grab something to drink or whatever while I run up and get changed," I said, skipping stairs two at a time.

I came back down, and Beth was at the kitchen sink refilling her water bottle. I could sense her melancholy.

"What's up? You seem upset," I probed as we started walking the bike trail.

"I'm just bummed. I've watched you come through your divorce with such a 'forgive and forget' attitude. I love going to your house. You are always ready to go and do. I wish *I* hadn't wasted so many years blaming my ex for everything. I want to *meet* someone. Your house is always so . . . happy . . . you have a beautiful daughter and *two* guys who want date you . . . people are always over, and I want that."

"Beth, 99 percent of getting what you want is knowing what you want. I think you finally know what you want. You need to focus your energy on getting it. And I really believe harboring hurt feelings only impedes your growth. I was so pissed off for so long that it just became exhausting to hang onto the anger. Once you let go of the negative and make room for the positive, your life just seems to transform overnight."

"How did you do it?" Beth asked.

"I don't think I *did* anything. I just I finally grew into the person I *wanted* to become. I was a kid when I got married. I claimed all his interests as mine because I didn't know any better. When it finally dawned on me that we wanted totally different things in life and that he had found someone to *share* his life with instead of *live* his life with, I was freed to pursue my own interests and enjoy *my* life. It's such a luxury to make my own choices instead of living with his, just because *he* knew what he wanted and *I* didn't."

"I hear you, but my ex destroyed my trust in men," said Beth.

"Sweetie, I'm only saying this because I love you, but you wear your anger like a badge. Your ex was a long time ago. He was only one man. The only person who is keeping you from trusting again is you. Once you *choose* happiness, you'll find it."

An hour later, when we walked back into the house, the phone was ringing, "Hey, Diane, I wanted to make sure you were home, is this a good time to come down?" Linda asked, which was odd because she usually knocks and walks in. Two minutes later, she walked in with my favorite, Breyers chocolate ice cream and a box of cones.

"This is a thank-you," she said, handing me the ice cream. "It all worked like a charm. Hey, Beth!"

I set the ice cream on the island and grabbed a spoon to dip. "Who wants a cone?" I asked as they both pulled up a chair for a cone.

Linda started telling her story to Beth from the beginning.

". . . And then, I called my friend, Carl, who is a cop, and he came over in his uniform and scared the hell out of Luke and the boys. He was so serious, *I* was cryin'. He was like 'Here your mom loves you so much and takes care of you, and this is how you boys repay her? Embarrassin' her in front of her neighbors? She doesn't deserve that. You are the men of this household; you need to step up, or you're goin' to find yourself in "juvie." And if that happens, your momma can't help you then.' Luke was just sittin' there speechless. By the time Carl was done with them, they were cryin' and apologizin' and grovelin' to me. It. Was. Great! My ex, Luke, took them around to the neighbors and made them apologize, and the boys are cleanin' flowerbeds as we speak," Linda laughed. "My ex thought my cop friend, Carl, was absolutely for real."

We took our cones to the back porch, and Beth said, "So is Carl cute and single?"

"He *is* cute, and I can find out if he's single," drawled Linda with a big smile.

I gave Beth a wink and thought, *Good for you!*

*   *   *

The next night when I pulled in the drive, my headlights lit up the front window, and I saw Jack! He was tall, with dark hair combed to the side with a part. He was standing with his hands in his pockets and maybe a dark sweater. It was such a brief glimpse, but I saw what Rose had been talking about. I was giddy with anticipation to see if I could still see him when I ran inside.

"Jack? I saw you in the window, I know you are here," I said to the living room in general.

"Women!" Jack sighed, frustrated.

"What? I just want to talk to you. Jack?" I asked, anticipating a reply. *Nothing.* "Men!" I said, equally frustrated.

The last thing I heard that night was the floorboard upstairs squeak.

A few weeks later, I saw the window open in the bathroom. "Jack?" *Nothing.* "I know you're there, I saw the window open, and I can smell your tobacco. I don't know why you are pouting."

I continued with my bedtime routine after changing into pajama pants and a tank top. I began brushing my teeth, when I felt a pinch to my behind. I jumped and jerked my head up, hitting it on the medicine cabinet mirror door, which had been ajar.

"*Ouch!* . . . Jack! . . . I know you did that!" I grabbed the brass knob on the window and turned the pane, locking it in place. When I entered my bedroom, the comforter and blankets had been turned down.

"What are you doing? I'm tired and not in the mood for your antics, Jack."

After I set the alarm with the remote, I turned off the lights, crawled into bed, and pulled the covers up around my neck. I was drifting on the edge of sleep when I felt the covers slipping down around my waist. I tucked them back around my neck and rolled over. Just as I fell into a state of sleep, I barely sensed a presence spooning me. It was comforting and allowed me to fall into a deep sleep.

The alarm clock started playing loud music at 5:30 a.m. I rolled over and turned off the alarm. As I stretched and pulled away the covers, I realized I was naked. *How does he do that?*

"Jack!" *Nothing.* I grabbed my robe and jumped into the shower to get ready for work. When I was washing my hair, I felt the gentle kneading of the warm water. As soap dripped down my body, so did the massaging warm water. I was enjoying the hot shower, until I felt the kneading creeping back up my legs and in between my thighs.

"Oh no, you don't!" I scolded. I quickly rinsed and turned off the shower. I was naked, combing through my wet hair in front of the mirror, when Jack appeared, sitting on the toilet with his legs crossed.

"Why do you do that?" asked Jack.

I nearly jumped out of my skin. I shrieked and dropped my comb while grabbing a towel. "What the hell? You don't at least knock or something?"

Jack knocked on the wall. "Satisfied?"

"Now you show up! Why didn't you ever answer me the countless times I *tried* to talk to you? I begged you to show yourself over and over," I said, perturbed, picking up my comb and finishing with my hair.

"You are the first woman who could see me; I wasn't sure of protocol. And I don't pout; I've been gone."

"Where were you?" I asked, curious.

"I went to the Middleton Tavern in Annapolis, Maryland. It's a favorite pub of the Naval Academy. I went there after you saw me in the window last night."

"That was two weeks ago; not last night."

"I don't measure time with clocks and calendars the way you do, but that explains why I was so tired last night," said Jack.

"So you don't have *any* concept of time?" I asked, as if I talk to ghosts every day while I'm getting ready for work.

"Time isn't something that I measure; it's something that I enjoy. When I'm tired of what I'm doing, I move on to something more interesting. I find *you* very interesting. Imagine my delight, when I came home and found you! It was a pleasant change from dogs, husbands, and kids. You have a striking resemblance to my fiancée, for whom I built this home. I find myself craving to come home to *you*."

"How did you take my clothes off?" I asked.

"I like sleeping with a naked woman. Why do you wear men's clothes to bed?" asked Jack.

"I don't wear men's clothes to bed, and I asked you *how* you took my clothes off," I said, agitated.

"Do you even own a nightgown? You wear men's pajama pants and an undershirt."

"I'm not taking fashion advice from you, Jack!" I said, frustrated.

The next second, he was gone. "Jack?" I asked the empty space.

Shit! Why didn't I ask him about the room in the attic?

"Jack! Wait!" I tried to call him back.

"Another time," answered Jack.

This is going to be interesting . . .

*   *   *

Later that week, I was enjoying a cup of coffee on the back porch when my thoughts drifted to the conversation I'd had the other day on the bike trail with Beth. It was hard to believe that just a year ago I had found out Don was cheating. I would never have believed it if someone had told me then that I would be moved on and happy in less than a year. It's so mind-boggling to realize how fast life can change. I realized that if you don't change with life's events, life just moves on without you. Holding on to anger and being unwilling to forgive stagnates you. When you are ready to forgive and let go of the pain, it's easy to relax with the flow of life. I had learned so much about myself when I accepted change and moved forward. It allowed me to live a more authentic lifestyle when I embraced life's uncertainties.

I had a much better understanding of the younger woman I was, and I was happy with the confident woman I had become.

I thought about the craziness of the soap opera on my block. Rose. Linda. Dale. Dorothy.

I thought about Beth and the camaraderie of the First Wives Club.

I thought about Jack, my ghost, and all my "encounters" with him, wondering what the future would be like coexisting with him.

I smiled at the thought of Mick, and my smile turned into a grin thinking of John.

The End